Other Books by Janet Tashjian

The Larry Series:
The Gospel According to Larry
Vote for Larry
Larry and the Meaning of Life

The My Life Series:
My Life as a Book
My Life as a Stuntboy

Fault Line
Marty Frye, Private Eye
Multiple Choice
Tru Confessions

FOR WHAT IT'S WORTH

A NOVEL

JANET TASHJIAN

with illustrations by Adam Gustavson

Christy Ottaviano Books
Henry Holt and Company
New York

A complete list of illustrations can be found at the end of the book.

Henry Holt and Company, LLC
Publishers since 1866
175 Fifth Avenue
New York, New York 10010
macteenbooks.com

Library of Congress Cataloging-in-Publication Data
Tashjian, Janet.
For what it's worth / Janet Tashjian. — 1st ed.
p.   cm.
"Christy Ottaviano Books."
Summary: Living in Los Angeles' Laurel Canyon neighborhood,
fourteen-year-old Quinn's life has been consumed by music and the
famous musicians who live nearby, but in 1971, his first girlfriend, a
substitute teacher, and a draft dodger help open his eyes about the
Vietnam War.
ISBN 978-0-8050-9365-0 (hc)
[1. Rock music—Fiction.   2. Musicians—Fiction.   3. Dating (Social
customs)—Fiction.   4. Family life—California—Los Angeles—
Fiction.   5. Teachers—Fiction.   6. Draft resisters—Fiction.
7. Vietnam War, 1961–1975—Fiction.   8. Los Angeles (Calif.)—
History—20th century—Fiction.]   I. Title.   II. Title: For what
it is worth.
PZ7.T211135For 2012
[Fic]—dc23

2011032001

First Edition—2012 / Designed by Elynn Cohen

Printed in the United States of America
10 9 8 7 6 5 4 3 2 1

For Doug and Jake—
with love, from me to you

Rock and roll can change the world and save your life—and that's just for starters. I challenge anyone on the planet to remain in a bad mood when "Gimme Shelter" comes on the radio. It's physically impossible, right? Rock and roll can get you through a boring school year, give you something to bond over with your friends, even provide you with a reason to get out of bed in the morning.

You think I'm exaggerating? Listening to music is a critical step in growing up, as important as learning how to ride a bike with no hands. And not just rock and roll—pop, rhythm and blues, country, jazz—I don't care what it is, I'll listen to it. I'm like a junkie with a twenty-four-hour addiction, except the needle's not in my arm, it's on my turntable. Lucky for me, I live in the epicenter of the national music scene. Not just California, but Los Angeles. And not just Los Angeles, but Laurel Canyon. If you love music, there's nowhere else to be in 1971 but here. I can sit on my front steps, throw a rock in any direction, and hit someone making music for a living. Songwriters, drummers, singers, sound engineers—I've trick-or-treated at their houses since grade school. My sister, Soosie, housesits for Joni Mitchell, for crying out loud. Don't believe me? Ask Soosie to show you the scratches on her arm from Joni's cat—the singer/songwriter might be known for writing emotionally bare songs about her love life, but her feline companion is a lot less subtle with her claws.

Where do I fit into this musical melting pot? I'm the guy who chronicles EVERYTHING in his ever-present notebook—Elton John's first U.S. appearance at the Troubador, The Band's newest demo, any rock-and-roll tidbit a music freak like me might want to know about. I continually make lists of songs, artists, and albums—mostly when I should be doing homework. I begged my English teacher last year to let me write a column for the school paper about the music scene called "For What It's Worth," based on the Buffalo Springfield song. She finally relented, and I've been cranking out columns and lists ever since. Just to keep in practice, I stockpiled several of them this summer too. Speaking of Joni Mitchell, I just finished one about her dumping Graham Nash while she was on vacation. Women—they'll annihilate your heart every time.

The city is pulsing, the city is moving to an internal beat—*can you hear it?*

I can.

My sister, Soosie, just got her hands on my journal—WHICH WAS IN MY ROOM, WHICH I ASKED HER FIFTY MILLION TIMES TO STAY OUT OF—and threw herself on her waterbed in a fit of convulsive laughter. If I gave the false impression that I knew what it actually felt like to lose a girlfriend, I apologize. Truth be told, I technically don't know what it's like to have one, never mind lose her. Ow! (My bilious older sister now has me in a headlock, insisting I be even MORE honest.) Okay! Not only have I never had a girlfriend, I haven't yet found a way to cross the chasm between the witty repartee in my head and a conversation with a real live human female that lasts longer than two seconds. My number one goal for this school year is to have a relationship with a smart, funny, pretty girl I can talk to. Happy now, Soosie? Sheesh. Go away to college already.

FOR WHAT IT'S WORTH

8/71

After a particularly domestic afternoon, Graham Nash wrote the song "Our House" about the Lookout Mountain home he shared with Joni Mitchell. The album the song was on--<u>Déjà vu</u>--had barely hit the airwaves when Mitchell split for Greece without him. While Nash was laying a new kitchen floor in the home they shared, he received a one-sentence telegram from Mitchell

informing him their relationship was over. Nash was crushed; he sat down at the same piano where he wrote "Our House" and wrote "Simple Man" about their breakup. It's almost as ironic as Joni writing "Woodstock"--the de facto anthem of the peace and love generation--from a Manhattan hotel room as she watched the coverage on TV.

While my parents are at work, I rummage through the garage until I find the long, curly brown wig Mom used to wear, then grab one of the scarves she sells in her store. I shut the door of my room and pull my Flying Burritos T-shirt over my head, exposing my bare chest, still tanned from the summer. I inspect myself in front of the mirror—neither my face nor chest has sprouted even the faintest hair. I adjust Mom's wig, tug my bell-bottoms a bit lower on my waist. But something's still missing for my spot-on Robert Plant impersonation, so I ignore Soosie's edict to stay out of her room—yes, I realize it's a double standard since I demand she keep out of mine—and grab a handful of silver bracelets from her bureau.

I stand in front of my turntable facing the toughest

decision of the day: "Dazed and Confused"? "Heartbreaker"? I decide to go with my old standby and crank up "Immigrant Song."

As Jimmy Page pounds out the opening riff, I jump around the room. *"A-ah-ahh-ah, ah-ah-ahh-ah!"* I stand in front of the mirror jangling the silver bangles on my arm and use the small piece of driftwood on my windowsill as a mic. *"To fight the horde, sing and cry: Valhalla, I am coming!"* I gyrate around the room, imagining thousands of fans singing along with me. It's as if one is actually in the room because a flash suddenly goes off, blinding me for a second.

"Who are you supposed to be?" Soosie asks. "Wait! Robert Plant? That's hilarious!" She fans the Polaroid picture in her hands.

"Give it to me!" I whip the wig off my head.

"Not on your life." She runs into the bathroom and gets the book of matches Mom keeps near the vanilla candles. She holds a lit match over her head. "Encore! Encore!"

"Why do you always take the best moments and WRECK them? Can you major in RUINING THINGS at Brandeis? 'Cuz you'd get all A's." I remove the bracelets from my arm and throw them at her one by one.

I shove her out of my room, but she remains in the hallway, laughing. "I'm going to miss you, Quinn," she adds.

"That makes one of us."

I shove my desk chair under the doorknob so she can't come in—what I should've done before I started my personal concert. I slide the Ouija board out from under my bed. My aunt Tamara gave this to me for my ninth birthday, but I started using it regularly only a few months ago. Yet another CONFESSIONAL TIDBIT: I'm superstitious, a sucker for any kind of portal to the other side. So is my aunt, which is why she gave me this present in the first place. I know it's meant for two people, but sharing this sacred game with Soosie is unthinkable. I place my fingers gently on the planchette. (Yes, that's what the plastic disc is called; check the instructions inside the box if you don't believe me.)

"How will it be when Soosie leaves?" I ask.

Y-O-U W-I-L-L B-E F-R-E-E, the Ouija responds.

You're telling me.

Outside the room, Soosie gives a long series of knocks that get exponentially louder until I can't take it anymore and open the door. She's written "Quinn, 8/20/71" on the bottom of the photo. In it I'm all limbs and hair, a whirling dervish streaking across the room. "Come on," she says. "Help me cook my going-away dinner."

My sister knows me well enough to realize I can't stay mad for long when food is involved. While Mom will point out a bag of noodles for me to boil, Soosie makes zucchini muffins and carrot and ginger soup. Watching Soosie chop fresh tomatoes and cucumbers now, I wonder how she's going to handle living in a small dorm room outside of Boston.

"No fresh herbs growing on windowsills all year long," I say. "No olive trees in the backyard."

As a way of shutting me up, Soosie hands me a clump of parsley to wash while Carole King's *Tapestry* fills the kitchen. The album came out a few months ago and has been in serious rotation with not only Soosie and me but our parents too. Soosie babysat for Carole's girls many times and was even in the room when Carole posed on the windowseat with her needlepoint for the album cover.

I make one last attempt to get Soosie to leave her comprehensive album collection here.

"Why do you think Melanie and I are driving instead of flying?" she answers. "I've got eight milk crates full!"

Mom bursts into the room carrying a platter of deli meat and cheese. "Here I am! Let the party begin!"

Mom's food is almost always inferior to anything Soosie makes, but she seems so eager to please, I tear off the plastic wrap and make several ham and Swiss roll-ups to tide me over till dinner.

Soosie places a large bowl of tabbouleh on the kitchen table with crackers artfully arranged on the side. I've been so worried about missing her music collection that I almost forgot about meals. What will I eat after tomorrow? Is this literally the Last Supper?

As if she knows what I'm thinking, Soosie hands me a cracker loaded with tabbouleh and tells me she'll send care packages from Boston.

"It's supposed to be the other way around," Mom says. "But I do have some going-away presents."

She hurries to the porch and returns with a giant bag of clothes. Mom opened her shop with imported clothes from India, then started designing dresses and blouses on her own. It didn't take long before she was running the busiest boutique on the Strip. Soosie has always been voted best dressed in her class at school; me, not so much.

Soosie oohs and ahhs as my mother pulls out dress after dress from her bag. "This one's made from a vintage tablecloth," Mom says. "This blue one has doilies for sleeves."

"I think she also needs goodies for the road." My father holds open the back door with his hip while carrying a large cardboard box full of trail mix, fruit, and bottles of juice.

Soosie is beaming—a guest would think my sister's happy because of all the gifts, but I know better. Soosie's pleased because both my parents are home and the four of us are together, a real rarity.

Dad moves a stack of books and puts his boots up on the table. He fixes cars at a high-end dealership in the Valley. After changing sparkplugs and overhauling engines all day, he usually retires to the garage to rebuild old radios and amps. He's much less gregarious than Mom, preferring to work with his hands than hobnob in the Canyon social scene. In all the years I've known him, I've never seen him without grease under his fingernails. He never talks about it, but he earned a Bronze Star for bravery when he fought in the Korean War.

The four of us spend the next few hours eating and telling stories until it's time for Soosie to pick up Melanie. We load the bags, albums, plants, food, and stereo into the back of her two-toned orange van—a trade-in from Dad's dealership that no one would buy so he fixed it up for Soosie.

"Call if you need *anything*, and I mean anything," Mom says in a blurry voice. I knew she shouldn't have opened that second bottle of wine.

"Change the world, make a difference, *contribute*," my father adds.

"Not too much pressure," I say.

Soosie rubs the top of my head the way she always has. "Come here, Mighty Quinn."

When she reaches over to give me a hug, she whispers in my ear. "I left you a present, but I'm not telling you where. By the time you find it, I'll be home for the holidays."

We wave goodbye until the van is out of sight. The sky teems with stars, and the air is filled with eucalyptus. It's the kind of Southern California night they write songs about. Here's the song I'd write tonight: *My sister's finally gone. Let my life and freedom begin!*

What? You think it's selfish that I don't want to stand in the shadow of my perfect older sister anymore? You don't know what it's like to have some Southern California poster girl with straight A's for a sister. The girl LITERALLY wears flowers in her hair. She can get backstage at the Whisky, the Troubador, any club in town. People *love* her. The Cowsills' "The Rain, the Park, and Other Things"? It was written for Soosie, I swear.

FOR WHAT IT'S WORTH

8/71

What do Linda Ronstadt, the Beatles, Dusty Springfield, the Monkees, the Drifters, the Everly Brothers, Aretha Franklin, the Chiffons, Marvin Gaye, Herman's Hermits, Manfred Mann, the Byrds, Laura Nyro, Dion and the Belmonts, the Four Seasons, the Animals, Skeeter Davis, and Blood, Sweat & Tears all have in common? They all recorded songs written by Carole

King with her now ex-husband Gerry
Goffin. Before she started recording on
her own, the woman was a songwriting
machine, even writing a #1 hit--"The
Loco-Motion"--for her teenage babysitter
to sing. King was barely out of her
teens herself when she wrote it. Her
song "Will You Love Me Tomorrow" was
recorded by lots of people, but the
Shirelles had a giant hit with it, the
first #1 on Billboard for a girl group
ever. If you've been to Carole's house
here in the Canyon, you'll know that's
the song that plays when you ring her
doorbell.

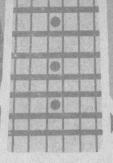

Great Summer Songs You'll Never Hear on the Radio After School Starts

★ "Summer in the City"—The Lovin' Spoonful

★ "Wipe Out"—The Surfaris

★ "Summertime"—Billy Stewart

★ "Summertime Blues"—Eddie Cochran

★ "Hot Fun in the Summertime"—Sly and the Family Stone

★ "In the Summertime"—Mungo Jerry

★ "Summer's Almost Gone"—The Doors

★ "All Summer Long"—The Beach Boys (Every Beach Boys song sounds like a summer song, although technically they're not. Did you know Brian Wilson, who wrote all those great beach songs, doesn't actually surf?)

When the Byrds heard the demo of Dylan's song "Mr. Tambourine Man," they decided they wanted to record it too. But their producer, Terry Melcher, didn't think the Byrds were strong enough to perform it. So he hired the Wrecking Crew to play on it—local guys who are the best studio musicians around. Besides the vocal harmonies, Roger McGuinn's twelve-string Rickenbacker is the only Byrds' music that's heard on the record. Their version of the song went to number one anyway, a first and only number one for Dylan. The record was credited with ushering in the whole folk rock genre, but besides McGuinn, the other guys hadn't played a note. Were they just happy for the monster single, or did they secretly wish they'd played on it too?

This is the kind of thing I think about when I'm lying in bed, stalling before getting up for breakfast.

When I run the Byrds conundrum by my mother, she takes a large sip from her mug of coffee before answering.

"This has nothing to do with 'Mr. Tambourine Man,'" she says. "You're worried about how the other kids will perceive you. Are you authentic or a phony? It's a perfectly understandable reaction to the first day of school."

My life has been a NIGHTMARE since my mother started psychoanalysis. I'm just glad I didn't bring up Captain Kirk's version of the song—I can only imagine the field day she'd have dissecting that one.

"You know, music trivia isn't the only way to connect with people," she continues. "You can ask someone what *they* want to talk about too."

If I don't take the bait, she won't quit and I'll never get to leave. "Okay, Mom. How are *you* doing today?"

She leans back and takes another sip of coffee. "I'm thinking about Soosie taking classes in Boston. I'm also thinking about how I'll be spending such a gorgeous morning dealing with vendors weeks behind schedule."

Sorry I asked. Mom gathers up the papers on the counter. "You want a ride to school?"

I tell her I'm meeting up with Ryan, even though I'm not. The last thing I need on the first day is my mom psychoanalyzing me in the car.

As I walk to school, I feel a stab of nostalgia for the loving cocoon of Wonderland Elementary. I went there years ago but used to love it—it was just a block from my house and I knew every kid there. At Bancroft, I not only have to leave an hour earlier but have to cross Hollywood, Sunset, and Santa Monica Boulevards. The streets are often littered with debris and more than once I've been hassled by a homeless guy on Fairfax. I usually end up giving him my lunch money because he seems to need it more than I do.

As much as I hate being back in school, it's great to see Willy and Ryan. Willy traveled to Mexico with his family, and Ryan spent the summer at his aunt's blueberry farm in the Berkshires. Because it would be long distance to call, we haven't spoken since school let out. We spend a few minutes catching up, but it doesn't take long before we get to THE GIANT NEWS OF THE SUMMER—how Jim Morrison died in Paris. The three of us used to see Jim and his girlfriend, Pamela, around the neighborhood because they lived behind the Canyon Store. For the past month, rumors swirled through town that Jim wasn't really dead since no one had seen his body except Pamela, who buried him in Paris before anyone else from the U.S. arrived.

"The doctor who signed the death certificate disappeared," Ryan says. "Morrison's probably sitting in some café in France laughing his butt off."

"How old was he?" Will asks. "Don't say twenty-seven."

"Yup," I answer.

"First Jimi, then Janis, now Jim," Ryan adds. "Club 27's recruiting new members all the time."

"Hey, don't forget Brian Jones," I say. "He started the club."

Ryan holds up his hand to stop me. "It's too early for your column—I'm still on vacation time."

Willy switches the conversation to the World Series and the three of us debate whether Baltimore will get a chance to defend their title. After a few minutes, he points to a girl sitting by the windows. "Who's the new kid?"

The girl in question wears what looks like a knit pantsuit. The closest I've seen to a getup like that is the outfit Janis Joplin wore while she belted out "Ball and Chain" at Monterey.

"Where'd she move from, Minnesota?" Ryan asks. "It'll be a hundred degrees by lunchtime—she'll bake like a sausage."

I can already see Lindy and Ashley snickering at the new kid from their seats. But I'm no longer focused on her clothes or short brown hair; what holds my attention is the black-and-white picture taped to the front of her binder. It's the photo of the girl screaming over the dead body of a student at Kent State.

As Mrs. Clarkson writes on the board, I run through an internal debate: hang out here with Willy and Ryan or actually have a conversation with the new girl? First off, she carries a notebook around like Yours Truly. (Yes, I know it's school and we all have notebooks, but hers seems particularly worn and comfortable, like the one I make lists and notes in for my column.) And second, it's got that gruesome Kent State photo on it, the same picture that Neil Young saw in *Life* magazine that inspired him to write the song "Ohio." I decide the musical coincidence is too much to ignore and weave my way through the desks, brushing off Willy's and Ryan's comments.

This year is going to be different. I can feel it.

I slide into the chair beside her. "Did you just move here?" I ask. Smooth, very smooth.

"From Connecticut." Her face blushes a deep pink. "I feel totally out of place."

"You'll love it. There's lots to do, that's for sure. My name's Quinn."

"Caroline."

I point to the notebook she now holds tightly to her chest. "That photo from the Kent State massacre—is that for a report?" Now THAT was stupid. How can she be doing a report on the first day of school?

She relaxes anyway and puts the notebook down. "Do you think it's morbid? It's one of my favorite photographs."

As she talks, I can see Willy and Ryan making fun of me behind Caroline's back.

"The guy who took this was in the student photo lab when he heard the commotion outside." Caroline becomes more animated and her red cheeks slowly fade. "He thought the National Guard was shooting blanks, but they were using real bullets. He was almost out of film when he took this shot."

I remember what my mother said this morning and try to broaden my subject matter. "It was a protest about the war, right?"

"The invasion of Cambodia," she adds.

Caroline is obviously a hundred times smarter than I am, but I try to keep up. I tell her my sister flew to DC five days after Kent State to join a demonstration of a hundred thousand people. I DIDN'T tell her Soosie wanted to initiate me into her world of activism by dragging me along but I chose to stay home to catch a glimpse of Zeppelin checking into the local Hyatt instead. That doesn't make me a bad person, does it?

"My brother flunked out of school last semester," Caroline continues. "He's nineteen—I hope he doesn't get drafted."

The conversation suddenly seems insanely heavy, so I try to lighten it up. "Is that what you like to do, take pictures?"

She reaches into the patchwork bag beside her desk

and takes out a camera. "I spent most of this summer in the darkroom."

"Sounds like torture." As I watch her face fall, I wish I could take the comment back. To change the subject, I motion to the girl in the picture. "Must've been horrible for her to watch her boyfriend get shot."

"She didn't even know him. She was our age, a runaway. Didn't go to Kent State."

"Really? She sure picked a bad day to pass through campus." Ashley and Lindy are now joining in the fun, four of my friends having a good old time goofing on me talking to the new girl in the strange clothes. But Caroline's so focused on our conversation, she doesn't notice.

I tell her how CSN&Y recorded "Ohio" quickly and less than three weeks later, it was playing on radios across the country.

"Really? I'll have to hear it sometime."

I jump out of my chair with so much force, I knock it to the floor. Ashley and Lindy burst out laughing. Smooth, Quinn—nice going.

I set my chair right and try to avoid another catastrophe. "You've never heard "Ohio"? It went to #14 on *Billboard*? "Find the Cost of Freedom" is the B-side?" I realize I'm getting carried away but can't control myself.

Caroline looks around, embarrassed the other

students are watching us. "I guess I'm a little behind on my music," she stammers.

Mrs. Clarkson finally finishes lining up the papers on her desk in ninety-degree angles and tells us to settle down. Her baby's not due for months, but her belly looks about to explode anyway. I head back to my seat between Willy and Ryan.

"What's your girlfriend's name?" Willy asks.

"We're going to bust your chops all day," Ryan adds.

I tell them both to shut up and slouch into my chair. Like a moron, I had to try and make some progress in my girlfriend quest ON THE VERY FIRST DAY OF SCHOOL. I couldn't have waited for a few days to get my footing? And this girl is SERIOUS. While I spend my days dissecting the lyrics to "I Am the Walrus," Caroline's worried about stuff going on in the outside world—just like my crazy sister. I mean, who wants to think about things like Vietnam if you don't have to? But maybe I did make a good impression on her. Maybe right now Caroline is drawing my name in the margins of her Kent State notebook, wondering when I'm going to make her day with another stimulating musical tidbit. I mean, it could happen, right?

Even I realize how delusional this train of thought is and get down to the real business at hand—revising my column on Club 27.

Be honest—it didn't go badly, did it? I mean, Caroline will talk to me again, right?

I can't tell anymore. I'm like a one-hit wonder with girls. A teenage Norman Greenbaum.

PLEASE tell me you get the reference.

And for those of you who disagree and say that "Spirit in the Sky" is not Norman Greenbaum's only hit, I say to you, "The Eggplant That Ate Chicago" and "Canned Ham" are novelty songs and don't count. I told you, I take this stuff SERIOUSLY. You should too if you're going to read my columns.

FOR WHAT IT'S WORTH

9/71

A few years ago--June 8, 1969, to be exact--Mick Jagger and Keith Richards visited Brian Jones at his home and kicked him out of the band he founded, which he named after glancing at an old Muddy Waters album. ("Rollin' Stone" didn't just influence the name of Jones's band--Dylan's "Like a Rolling Stone," Hendrix's "Voodoo Chile," and the infamous rock magazine all were homages to Muddy's song.)

Less than a month after getting booted from the band, Brian Jones  drowned in his swimming pool at the same country estate where A. A. Milne of Winnie-the-Pooh fame used to live. He was Club 27's first member, if you don't count blues legend Robert Johnson, who died in 1938 of strychnine poisoning at that age too. I'm usually not superstitious, but 27 is NOT my favorite number.

Because Ryan is a giant Doors fan, he suggests we spend Saturday paying tribute to Jim Morrison. Willy opts for surfing in Santa Monica, but I happily oblige. I just hadn't planned on Ryan's enthusiasm; he rustles me out of bed Saturday morning with a full itinerary. I throw on some clothes and leave my parents a note.

I haven't been downtown since last winter when my Dad and I went to check out the damage from the 6.5 earthquake that killed sixty-five people. The windows of almost every storefront on Broadway had blown out, and the pavement glistened with shards of glass. We picked our way around police barricades, grateful our home had been spared. As Ryan and I descend from the bus today, we almost have Hope Street to ourselves.

I pull out a tasty tidbit from my column on the

Doors. "You know 'Mr. Mojo Risin'' is an anagram for Jim Morrison, right?"

"I knew that *before* I read your column." Ryan laughs. "Let's get something to eat."

We find a doughnut shop on the corner where we're lucky enough to catch the woman taking a tray of glazed doughnuts out of the oven. *Bacon* doughnuts.

"I don't think I've ever had a bacon doughnut before," Ryan says. "Why didn't somebody combine these two a long time ago?"

"Never mind bacon—I've never had a *warm* doughnut," I answer with my mouth full.

We order an extra two for the road, which we end up eating before we leave the shop. Then we head to our destination: the Morrison Hotel. When Ryan asks a mailman to take our picture out front, he begrudgingly agrees.

"The guy behind the desk told the band they couldn't pose in the lobby," Ryan says. "So when the clerk went upstairs, the Doors hurried inside and their photographer shot a few photos from the street."

I nod as if I don't know this piece of album cover trivia, hadn't written about it in my column, oh, I don't know, LAST YEAR. I keep my mouth shut though, because between the two of us, Ryan is the real Doors fan so I'm happy to let him be the expert today. We hang around downtown for another half hour then catch a different bus to Venice Beach.

Whether it's because he's an only child or because his parents are divorced, Ryan's always had more freedom than I have. I don't know any other kid with divorced parents, so I'm curious about how things work with two separate households. But even though he's my best friend, I'm too uncomfortable to ask for details, so we spend the ride talking about how Ryan just painted his bedroom at his dad's place black and got UV lights to show off his black-light posters. It's like a psychedelic music den that he insists makes his albums sound a hundred times better, and based on listening to Grand Funk's *Closer to Home* the other day, I have to agree with him.

It's eighty-eight degrees by the time we get to Venice so we go straight to the beach. The boardwalk is full of tattoo artists, tourists, and hustlers.

"This is the year we start a band." Ryan picks up an empty soda bottle, pretends it's a microphone, and feigns a Lizard King pose. Two little girls in bathing suits walk by and laugh.

"I play guitar and transcribe music. You play three chords and wear vinyl pants—not even leather ones. Great band we'd make."

Ryan tosses a handful of sand in my direction. "It's still the best way to meet girls."

As much as I love jamming with Ryan, we come at music from two different places. For Ryan, music is a basic pleasure as enjoyable as those warm doughnuts resting inside my stomach. Of *course* music is fun—nothing brings a grin to my face faster than nailing an elusive chord for the first time—but it's more than that too. For me, there's an internal structure, a language I want to be a part of. I care more about how Ray Manzarek played bass on the keyboards than I do about Morrison's drunken theatrics.

Ryan and I walk around the boardwalk and more than once, I miss Soosie's protective presence. Not that the area is dangerous this time of day, but it's a part of town I've never been to with just a friend. Later, we split a plate of ribs at Olivia's Kitchen, the small restaurant Morrison based "Soul Kitchen" on. Walking back to the bus stop, I grab Ryan's arm.

"What is *that*?"

He and I stare at a kid our age cruising down the boardwalk on a piece of wood with wheels. The kid wears a huge smile as he weaves through the pedestrian traffic.

"No idea, but it looks like he's having a blast," Ryan answers.

On the bus home, I think about how big the city is, how each section of Los Angeles has its own personality and tribe. You don't have to be someone who's lived here forever to notice the differences between Hollywood and Sunset Boulevards—and they're only a block apart. Even though I'm a native Angeleno, there are so many parts of the city I haven't discovered yet. As much as I love knowing a wild and diverse city awaits, I also take comfort in the fact that I can call the cozy Canyon home.

We take photos of the Alta Cienega Motel, where Morrison lived in room 32 for a while. Outside the Whisky a Go Go—where the Doors made their groundbreaking debut that got them a record contract—a few other people take pictures.

"Tourists," Ryan mutters underneath his breath.

"They're probably paying tribute to Morrison too."

"It's different," Ryan continues. "We live here, we knew him. He used to talk to us."

I burst out laughing. Morrison talked to us ONCE, a few years ago when we skidded on our bikes and nearly crashed into him walking up Lookout Mountain Avenue. He looked like he'd been wearing the same clothes for days and swore at us as he stumbled back up the road. Even in the broadest definition of the word *relationship*, we didn't have one with Morrison. My mother, however, gave lots of advice to Morrison's girlfriend, Pamela, when she set up her own boutique on La Cienega. Mom never looks at other people opening stores as competition; her philosophy is always inclusive and communal.

Ryan elbows me again. "Well, look who's here—your new girlfriend."

I don't know who he's talking about until I see Caroline come out of a bookstore with an older woman, probably her mother.

"Look what's she's *wearing*!" Ryan says. "Is she insane?"

Caroline sees us and waves self-consciously. She has on a pleated navy blue skirt, but that's not the worst of it. What I can't get my head around is that it matches her mother's. I want to die of embarrassment to save her the trouble.

She introduces us to her mom, who shakes our hands. I can tell from Caroline's face that she's horrified she ran into us and I pray Ryan doesn't make this chance encounter harder for her than it has to be. We tell her about our Doors day.

"I love 'Riders on the Storm,' " she says. "I love the sound of the rain." She seems proud to have more musical knowledge than our last conversation.

"Are you two out on your own in a city this size?" Caroline's mother asks.

"We grew up here," Ryan answers. "It's kind of our neighborhood."

I decide not to throw in the added detail that we just got back from Venice Beach and that I left my parents a note telling them where I was while they were still asleep. Thinking of my mom gives me an idea.

"You should check out my mother's shop." I point down the street. "It's only two blocks down—it's the best clothing store in the city."

Caroline looks at her mother imploringly.

"Tell her you're a friend of mine and she'll definitely give you a discount," I say.

Caroline's face lights up, and I wonder if it's because of the discount or that I just referred to her as a friend. Do I sound like a moron if I hope it's the latter?

"She may not have that many mother/daughter outfits, but she does have good stuff," Ryan adds.

I want to bash Ryan with his own camera as I watch Caroline's smile deflate.

"Let's do it," her mom says. "We definitely need some new duds."

I give them directions then turn to Ryan when we're alone.

"Duds?" he says. "What in the world are duds?"

"*You're* a dud," I say. "Why'd you have to make her feel worse than she already did?"

"Sorry I insulted your girlfriend," he says. "Come on, we have one more stop."

As we head to Santa Monica Boulevard, I look over my shoulder to watch Caroline and her mom. The last thing I want to do is hang around my mother's store while a girl I barely know tries on clothes, but part of me also wishes Ryan would hurry up and finish with his tribute already.

Even with Morrison gone, the Doors' office and studio bustle with activity. I heard a rumor that the surviving members of the band were making another album without him; turns out it was true. Robby and Ray split the lead singer duties and the album comes out next month. The receptionist downstairs waves us in when we tell her we want to take a photo of the bathroom. I guess lots of other Doors fans have already made the same pilgrimage.

Morrison recorded one of the Doors' very best songs—"L. A. Woman"—in the bathroom here in one take. Jim thought he could get a fuller sound there and he was right. Soosie and I always raced for the volume knob on the car radio whenever the song came on. It isn't just that the song is about our town—it *rocks*. I remember being in Soosie's van with three of her friends, all four of them singing at the top of their lungs, windows open, not caring one bit about the businessman at the red light shaking his head and laughing. *"Are you a lucky little lady in the City of Light?"* I sat in the backseat singing too, taking in the scene as a window into the secret lives of girls.

I snap a photo of Ryan sitting on the toilet seat as if he's also making a hit record there.

"I know Morrison was a mess," Ryan says as we walk home, "but I'm still really sorry he's gone."

Maybe because it's Caroline's favorite, but I can't get the eerie thunder and rain opening of "Riders on the Storm" out of my mind. The day that album came out last spring, Ryan raced into my house and insisted I listen to that track right then and there. It was rainy that afternoon—a rarity in L.A.—and the song matched the ominous skies perfectly, an uncanny combination of life meeting art head on. It seemed as if it were written for that exact moment, just for us. When the song finished, Ryan turned the album over and played the other side while the two of us sat on the braided rug taking it all in. This is what I can't explain, how there's so much more to music than forming a band for the sole purpose of attracting screaming fans. How those moments of *bonding* with a song are holy—dare I say it?—even one of the reasons we're here. The rainy afternoon Ryan turned me onto that song is etched into my being forever, part of my musical DNA. I get another idea for a column and race home to write it, NOT just to see if Caroline stopped by my mother's store.

know what you're thinking—isn't this the same guy who was hopping around like Robert Plant a few weeks ago? Why so high and mighty all of a sudden?

And to you I say, "Guilty as charged." That being said, I meant every word about music saving your life, music being sacred. I believe in that 100 percent. So what's wrong with adding a few screaming girls into the mix?

Speaking of girls, I know it doesn't make any sense, but there's something cool about Caroline being so uncool. Just because she's not in bell-bottoms and plat-form sandals like the rest of the girls at school doesn't mean she's any less smart or fun than they are. It's like the list I keep in the back of my notebook: "Songs I'm Afraid to Admit I Like." Everybody has those, right? The ones you make fun of in front of your friends but never switch the station when they come on the radio? I just added one to my list last week—"Superstar" by the Carpenters. I give my mother such grief when she listens to them belting out their stupid ballads on the radio, but THAT song? You have to admit it's kind of great. And it's not just because the backstory is filled with artists of real credibility—it was written by Leon Russell and Bonnie Bramlett about some fictional groupie pining after their buddy Eric Clapton—but also because of the arrangement itself. I mean, who opens a pop song with a stinking OBOE? And a female singer with over-the-top histrionics who plays drums? The song should SUCK, but it doesn't. That's what I'm saying about Caroline—kneesocks and a pleated skirt that matches her mother's? Sure, it SOUNDS terrible, but who knows? Maybe there's a sleeper hit in there somewhere too.

FOR WHAT IT'S WORTH

9/71

Ray Manzarek knew Jim Morrison from a
film class at UCLA. When he ran into
Morrison at Venice Beach, Morrison sang
him the lyrics to a poem he'd written
called "Moonlight Drive." Manzarek said
they should form a band and asked a
guy from his Transcendental Meditation
class if he wanted to join. John
Densmore brought his friend Robby
Krieger, and the Doors were born. It

couldn't have been more random or
spontaneous. Suppose Manzarek hadn't
been at the beach that day, suppose
Densmore never meditated? All that
music, gone. All those memories of
mine, of yours--poof! It almost makes
you believe in destiny.

My mother gives me two earfuls of grief the second I walk in the door. I tell her I looked for a pay phone several times during the day but couldn't find one. It turns out she's not the only one who's upset.

"It's okay for you to take the bus with a friend," my father says, "but downtown? You were a block from Skid Row!"

For the tenth time, I tell him Ryan and I were fine.

"Almost three million people live in this city," he continues. "That guarantees more than a few creeps."

He doesn't have to spell it out more than that; we all know who he's referring to. Even though the Charles Manson murders took place two years ago, the city still reverberates with their after effects. People who used to leave their doors open all the time began locking them.

Canyon residents started to check out partygoers on their patios and porches. Dad didn't have to mention the fact that Susan Atkins—one of Manson's "family"—had been to our house several times. My parents still can't talk about the fact that Susan actually watched me one afternoon while Mom tended to the store. Dad doesn't need to say it, but I know his concern about Ryan and me going downtown today is the memory of the freak show of a trial that took place in the courthouse there last summer. My parents were understandably rocked by the whole affair, enough to change all the locks in the house and install several deadbolts, which we used for a month or two before resorting to our standard open-door policy.

My mother steers the conversation to another topic. "Your new friend came into the store today. Caroline? Very nice."

"I told her to ask for a discount—was that okay?"

She hands me a slice of pear. "She and her mother picked out several pieces. I was happy to give them a discount."

I wait for her to mention the mother/daughter outfits but she doesn't.

"I don't think they know a soul in town. You should have Caroline over sometime."

I shrug, even though I was planning to do just that.

As if she can feel my conversational discomfort three

thousand miles away, Soosie calls. She's been gone a month, and I finally wrote her my first letter the other day because my mom told me we couldn't afford the collect phone calls. My father waits patiently as Mom asks Soosie about her classes; I hope talking to Soosie will put an end to Dad's concerns about how dangerous the city can be.

After my father finishes with Soosie, he hands the phone to me. I tell my sister about my day with Ryan, and she laughs.

"You went to Venice by yourselves? What, are you all grown up now?" She asks me how school's been and if I've been practicing guitar.

I suddenly realize that we've been on the phone for almost ten minutes. "Don't you have to go? This will cost more money than a plane ticket home."

Her voice shifts to a whisper. "I just found out about this new trick you can do with phones—it's called phreaking."

She explains that some enterprising guy discovered that the whistle that comes inside a box of Cap'n Crunch cereal just happens to blow at a frequency of 2600 hertz—the same one the phone company uses to change trunk lines. "If you blow it into the phone, you can make long distance calls for free."

"The Cap'n Crunch whistle—are you kidding me? How does someone discover something so random? Did he go through every toy in a box of Cracker Jacks first? Besides, you *hate* Cap'n Crunch."

"Not anymore! But don't tell Mom and Dad, okay? It's illegal."

I'm so fascinated with someone coming up with something so arbitrary that it almost doesn't dawn on me that this is obviously some kind of theft.

"You should get one and try it," she says. "That way you can call me whenever you want for nothing."

"And why would I do that?'

"Did you find the present I left you yet?"

I tell her I tore apart both our rooms and the den but came up empty-handed. Before I hang up, she makes me promise to call using her new system.

As Mom thumbs through a stack of magazines, I try to look nonchalant as I take down the box of Cap'n Crunch from the top shelf of the cupboard and pour myself a bowl.

"You still hungry?" she asks.

I tell her just a little and head to my room with the box and bowl. I spend most of the night calling in requests to KHJ and trying to put my music trivia knowledge to good use by winning free tickets to see the new singer-songwriter Jackson Browne. I go back and forth between the AM and FM dials, listening to several cuts by Yes on KLOS as I finish the cereal.

Deep inside the box is the prize—nothing special,

just a cheap plastic whistle. When I blow it, it makes the same sound these whistles have always made. The question is: Am I brave enough to blow it into the phone to find out if Soosie's scheme works?

I want to tell Ryan and Willy right away—long-distance crank calls!—but my mom's back on the phone with one of her friends. If I do try the new system, will several cops come bursting through the door as soon as the other person picks up? Maybe if I just *receive* illegal phone calls, I won't be breaking any laws and Soosie will be the one to get caught.

I reach under my bed and slide out my Ouija board. (I don't even bother keeping it in the box anymore.) "Should I use the whistle?"

This time there are no letters to string together; my hand slides across the board to the word **YES**. Hopefully the Ouija gods won't rat me out to the phone company or the cops. I slip the plastic whistle into the top drawer of my desk, then lift the bowl to my mouth and drink the sugary orange milk left behind.

Okay, here's the question: If you could call someone long distance for free, who would it be?

I don't think I've ever even made a long-distance call; this might take some thought . . . *Rolling Stone* in San Francisco or *CREEM* in Detroit, to try and talk them into printing some of my columns? Where is Lester Bangs—should I try and call him? Or maybe Ryan when he's in the Berkshires next summer?

When I really stop and think about it, I don't know that many people outside of Laurel Canyon. But here's an idea—maybe I can impress Caroline with my phreaking skills and let her call her friends back in Connecticut for free.

Thank you, Captain Crunch.

FOR WHAT IT'S WORTH

10/71

Lots of people in this town were taken in by Charles Manson and his entourage. Before the murders, he was just another longhaired, bearded songwriter hanging around the Canyon. The Beach Boys even recorded one of Manson's songs: "Never Learn Not to Love." Dennis Wilson is credited on the album, but it's Manson's song all the way. The rumor is, Manson wanted to kill Terry Melcher--the

bigwig producer who is also Doris Day's
son--for not giving him a record deal
but didn't know he'd moved to Malibu.
Poor Sharon Tate was unlucky enough to
be renting Melcher's old Benedict
Canyon house instead. (She was 26, not
27; I checked.)

I almost don't recognize Caroline when I see her at school on Monday. Her jeans have so many patches, they look like Neil Young's pair on *After the Gold Rush*. Her peasant blouse is definitely from Mom's store—my sister has one exactly like it. I'm not the only guy who notices; Ryan raises his eyebrows and grins when he sees her too.

"Your mom's the best," Caroline says. "She even talked mine into getting two dresses to replace the dumb pantsuits she always wears."

I look around to make sure Ryan isn't still lurking behind his locker to hear this conversation about clothes.

"It's a great store," she continues. "I'm definitely going back."

I hadn't noticed before but Caroline's brown eyes are flecked with bits of green, almost like stained glass.

"She said I should come over sometime, that you have a great record collection."

I tell her I do and stammer that I'm around most afternoons. That's the moment when I notice Willy laughing in the hall. I tell Caroline I have to go then pounce on him when she's not looking.

Mrs. Clarkson says her doctor insists on bed rest for the final months of her pregnancy so we'll be having substitute teachers sooner than she thought. While half of the class—mostly girls—wish her well with the baby, the others—like my friends and me—plot what we can get away with while she's gone.

After school, I ask Ryan and Willy if they want to practice at my house. Ryan can't because he has an orthodontist appointment and Willy's heading to Malibu to surf. I shrug and tell them I'm playing anyway.

I'm halfway through the opening riff of Shocking Blue's "Venus" when I hear someone at the door. I unplug my guitar and am stunned to see Caroline on the porch with her camera swinging around her neck. I stare at her blankly.

"You said I should come over sometime."

"I didn't think we were talking about TODAY." I berate myself for making her smile crumple yet again and—more important—sabotaging the first girl that's been over here who isn't a family friend. "Actually, today is fine," I say. "Come on in." I offer her some grapes and show her around the house.

"We live in a bungalow too," she says. "The insurance company in Hartford where my dad works rented it for us while he opens up a new office here."

Like a good potential boyfriend, I store all this boring information for later use.

She motions to my guitar and asks what I was playing so I plug the guitar back into the amp and finish the song.

"That was great. What else can you play?"

"I can make my way on piano, but I really prefer guitar."

She laughs. "I mean what other *songs*?"

I laugh too and launch into "Heart Full of Soul" by the Yardbirds. In a million years, I'd never compare my skills to Jeff Beck's, but it's one of the only songs I can play with virtually no mistakes.

Except this time.

When my fingers slide to B instead of D, my grimace gives me away. But Caroline encourages me to keep going. I finish up the rest of the song, thankfully with no more errors. "It would sound better if I had a fuzz box," I explain.

"What are you talking about? You were amazing."

I put the guitar back in its stand and opt for a safer route—my record collection. I sit on the floor next to Caroline, who asks how many albums I have.

"Three hundred seventy-eight."

"Wow!"

"Counting double albums as one, of course."

"Of course."

I try to decide if she's making fun of me, but her next comment tells me she is. "They're in alphabetical order!"

"Would you rather I just throw them around the room?"

"How can you afford all these?"

I explain that every penny of my allowance, every chore I do around the neighborhood, every dollar I receive for birthdays and holidays gets plowed right into my record fund.

She suddenly squeals as if she just spotted David Cassidy outside by the compost bin. (Don't get me started on him—PLEASE!)

"Play this! Play this!" She holds up a copy of Joni Mitchell's *Blue*, an undeniable breakthrough record but as depressing as a vinyl platter can possibly be. I drag the other beanbag chair out of Soosie's room and plop on the floor next to Caroline, who's already transfixed by the hypnotic combination of Mitchell's poetry and open tunings. Ryan calls Mitchell the Pied Piper of girls and I agree with him.

"I like *Ladies of the Canyon* too," I start to say before Caroline shushes me back to silence. I want to tell her my mom is friends with the women Joni wrote about in the title song, but it hardly seems worth interrupting Caroline's musical rapture. I stare at the post-and-beam ceiling and settle in for a serious dose of after-school melancholy.

When side one ends, I race to the turntable and pull off the record. Caroline is visibly disappointed. "I have to head home anyway, thanks for letting me see your collection." She gently holds the album cover as if it's made of hand-blown glass.

"The guy who took the photograph was one of the original actors on *My Three Sons*." I personally think this is a fun piece of trivia, but Caroline bursts into laughter.

"How do you *know* this stuff?"

"It's interesting to me—the stuff I write about in my column."

She tilts her head and scrunches up her nose and I decide Caroline is the most adorable girl in our class.

"You should stop by the paper after school," I continue. "Maybe Patty—she's the editor—can use some of your photographs."

"I think I will." She holds up the album like a waiter presenting a tray of delicacies. "We haven't known each other that long but I'm someone who *really* takes care of things. Is there any way I can borrow this? I won't scratch it, I promise."

I suddenly wonder if the tilted head and scrunched-up nose were part of a premeditated ploy to forage through my record collection. What Caroline doesn't know is that after Willy scratched the snot out of one of my Janis Joplins and destroyed my Creedence Clearwater, I NEVER let people borrow records anymore.

I obviously take too long answering because Caroline reneges on her request and puts the album back. I can't help but smile when she places it in its correct spot. I grab the album again and hand it to her. "Definitely take it. I won't play it again this week anyway."

Her face lights up and before I can stop her, she lifts up her camera and snaps a photo of me.

"Hey!"

"I'll show it to you after I develop it. And I promise to take good care of *Blue*."

I spend the rest of the afternoon writing my report on Julius Caesar and wondering how goofy I'll look in Caroline's picture.

finally get up the nerve to blow the whistle into the phone. I'd be lying if I told you I'm not nervous because I am. The last thing I want is for Soosie to torture me about having a girl finally come over to our house so I wait till she's about to hang up before I tell her. She laughs so hard, I'm afraid she's having a seizure.

"It's about time," she finally says.

I tell her it's no big deal, but of course it is.

As big as the Beatles breaking up. But in a good way this time.

FOR WHAT IT'S WORTH

10/71

My sister and I were standing behind
the police barricades at the Landmark
Motel when they removed Janis Joplin's
body last summer. Several other people
OD'd that week--the newspaper said there
was a bad bunch of heroin going around--
but poor Janis died alone, her
psychedelic Porsche convertible outside
in the parking lot. When she bought it,
the car was oyster white; one of her

roadies gave the car its multicolored paint job. The car was so distinctive that fans used to leave notes for Janis underneath the windshield wipers when they saw it around town. Seeing the car in the motel lot as the medical examiner wheeled Janis's body away was almost like watching a dog or cat left behind, still waiting for its owner. Two days after she died, John Lennon received a cassette in the mail with Janis singing Dale Evans's "Happy Trails" to wish him a happy 30th birthday. Creepy, right?

Soosie's latest letter talks about a nice guy working at the campus deli who just got drafted.

"Your sister and her friends tried to sign him up for classes to get a college deferment but it didn't work," Mom says. "I guess they're all pretty upset by it. Sounds like she's already made some good friends." Mom leaves the letter on the counter for Dad to read later.

"Oh, I almost forgot to give this to you." She hands me a small box. Inside is a pair of earrings made of peacock feathers. I stare at her blankly.

"You want me to pierce my ears?"

"They're for your friend Caroline! I just got them in and I thought they'd match the outfit she bought."

I realize Mom is being thoughtful and generous, but all I can think about is how can I possibly give them to

Caroline without being tortured for the rest of my life by my friends? Luckily, when I get to school, the substitute teacher solves my problem by telling us to work in pairs and assigning Caroline to me.

Caroline drags her desk over and motions to the new teacher. "She wrote *Ms.* Thompson on the board—what does *that* mean?"

I tell her I don't have a clue and quietly shove the small box across the desk.

"Is this a present?"

"From my mom—she wanted me to give it to you."

"So you're just the messenger?" Caroline looks about to smile. It was easier talking to her when she was new at school and afraid of everything. I'm not sure I like this flirty new confidence.

"Just the messenger," I agree.

"I'll trade you." She slides an eight-by-ten black-and-white photo across the desk. It's the photo she took at my house last week. I'm near my stereo and smiling. Besides the smattering of freckles I still get embarrassed about, I almost look handsome.

"You can keep it," she says. "I made two."

"You can't keep one!" I'm not sure why I sound so defiant because I'm actually flattered she wants one for herself.

Caroline waits until Ms. Thompson—or whatever she

calls herself—finishes giving instructions, then lowers the box behind her desk to open it. She can barely contain her excitement.

"These are amazing," she says. "Tell your mom thanks so much." She raises her hand and asks if she can go to the restroom then returns minutes later with the blue and green feathers dangling from her ears.

Willy shoots me a look that says, *What is going on over there?* I shoot one back that says, *Nothing!* We spend the next half hour making notes on the Roman Empire while Caroline gently caresses her latest treasured possession.

When she gathers up her things after class, I spot the Kent State photo on her binder and ask her if she's heard "Ohio" yet.

She looks at me for a few moments and I'm shocked to see her eyes overflow with tears.

"It's okay if you haven't listened to it," I stammer. "Music isn't the most important thing." I CAN'T BELIEVE THAT SENTENCE JUST CAME OUT OF MY MOUTH.

She looks around to make sure no one is watching then wipes her eyes with the back of her hand. "Remember the draft in August?"

I nod as if I do.

"My brother's birthday was one of the first days they picked. He tried to get out of it, but he's getting inducted."

Of course she's not crying over CSN&Y, you numbskull—her brother got DRAFTED. I've never had a prospective girlfriend before, let alone one who's crying. What do I do? I reach across the desk for her hand, hoping that will comfort her in some simple way.

"He's shipping out next week," she continues. "My father says if Billy hadn't flunked out, this never would've happened. My mother doesn't want him to get hurt."

I know the draft works on a lottery system—I guess I just never thought of how unlucky it is for the kids who get picked first. I wonder if Caroline's brother has the same birthday as Soosie's friend back in Boston.

Caroline is obviously used to the role of good girl, because she composes herself and pulls her hand away from mine the instant the bell rings. "I'll definitely listen to 'Ohio.' Maybe you'll even let me borrow it."

I'm in awe of her memory too, picking up the conversation exactly where we left off. I tell her I hope her brother will be okay; I also tell her "Ohio" isn't on an album yet but she can borrow the 45.

Ryan overhears me on his way out of the classroom. "I see the lending library has reopened—I'll be coming by for those Dead albums you wouldn't let me borrow. I'll tell Willy you're back in business too."

Ryan has me over a barrel and knows it. I retaliate

by telling him Jerry Garcia plays long, boring guitar solos, which sends him jumping over the desk to strangle me. Ms. Thompson tells him to calm down and I realize my anti-Dead comment probably means Ryan will try to borrow as many albums as he can carry tonight.

There should be some kind of operating manual vis-à-vis friends and albums, am I right? I mean, just because you jump off tire swings into a lake with a kid doesn't mean he gets to scratch your John Mayall, spill soda on the liner notes to Emerson Lake & Palmer, or warp your *Pet Sounds* by leaving it in the back seat of his parents' car—right, Willy? He's too cheap to buy a new needle, so when his records started skipping, Willy taped a dime to the arm of his turntable and when THAT didn't work, he added a nickel.

What's a nickel weigh? I'm too lazy to go to the library and look it up, but whatever it is, I guarantee it's too heavy for those delicate grooves.

But here's the worst—one of Soosie's friends actually

borrowed my *Woodstock* soundtrack, wrapped the cover in aluminum foil, and then tried to get a tan on her face IN MY BACKYARD by using it as a sun reflector. ARE YOU KIDDING ME? A record is FRAGILE. Show some respect.

FOR WHAT IT'S WORTH

10/71

Jerry Garcia, famous for his ambitious--
aka long--guitar solos, plays with only
a partial middle finger on his right
hand. He lost it when he was just four
years old, while helping his brother
chop wood and his brother lost control
of the ax. A year later, Garcia watched
from the shore as his father drowned
while fly-fishing. And when he was

eighteen, Garcia got into a car
accident that killed one of his best
friends. I hope that kind of cumulative
tragedy isn't a prerequisite to being a
good guitarist.

For the next week, my mother constantly talks about the "breakthrough" she made in her therapy session. Her psychoanalyst suggested keeping a dream journal and Mom now spends every morning before work either vigorously writing or talking intently on the kitchen phone with her friends. One of her dreams gave her insight as to why she and Grandma still fight about the same things over and over like some ancestral Möbius strip. I don't think you need a dream to tell you that Grandma can be nasty; it seems to me that she picks fights with Mom on every one of our visits. But if some dream can help Mom deal with her ornery mother, I guess it's better than fighting all the time.

Several neighbors with younger kids get in the spirit of Halloween by decorating the front of their houses with pumpkins and scarecrows. Soosie and I used to love walking through the Canyon at night, carting around pillowcases stuffed with candy apples and popcorn. Last year Ryan, Willy, and I didn't dress up but went around to people we knew for candy anyway.

I finish my math homework, then dig out my fine black marker and notebook. I've wanted to transcribe the music to "Can't You Hear Me Knocking" all week and can't wait to start. How does Keith Richards come up with all these amazing opening riffs? My parents got me *Sticky Fingers* for my birthday; with the photo of the jeans and its real movable zipper, the album cover is one of my favorites. Soosie said Andy Warhol designed it. (The only reason I know Warhol's name is because he designed the banana on the cover of *The Velvet Underground & Nico*, and the first time I saw his signature on the front of the album, I thought Andy Warhol was the name of the band.)

I learned the song on guitar a few months ago but still feel more comfortable when I have sheet music in front of me. It's not that I read the music when I'm playing—I just learn any song more quickly after I've transcribed it note for note. It's a finicky habit that works for me.

Using the ruler, I draw five lines across the page then make several more groupings till I hit the bottom of the notebook. Of course I didn't compose any of the songs

I transcribe, but listening to them carefully and writing down each note makes me feel closer to the creative process. Mom says I remind her of a monk in the Dark Ages hand-copying books to preserve them. Dad is just happy to see me at my desk.

I draw the bar line, G clef, key and time signatures, then fill in the first several notes from memory. When I press the marker against the paper, the ink spreads and fills in the inside of each note. Then I put on the album and play the next few bars. G-D-G-D-G-B-D. It's a tedious process to get through a whole song this way, but for some reason this is one of the only tasks where I have all the patience in the world. Forty-five minutes go by and I only look up when I hear someone at the back door.

Caroline holds *Blue* in one hand and a plate of brownies with walnuts in the other. She wears the earrings from my mom, and her ever-present camera is around her neck.

I take the album out and examine it. (I don't mention the fact that she's had the record WAY too long.) "Well, you take better care of records than Willy, that's for sure."

"Does that mean I get to borrow another one?" Caroline offers me a brownie. It might be a bribe, but I grab one anyway and invite her inside.

In homage to Duane Allman, who just died—motorcycle accident, not drugs; age twenty-four, not twenty-seven—I grab my guitar and launch into an amateur version of "Midnight Rider." When I finish, I give poor Duane an informal eulogy and am shocked at Caroline's lack of knowledge of one of rock's great guitarists.

"You didn't know he was one of the dueling guitars on *Layla?*" I ask incredulously.

"I thought it was just Eric Clapton."

"Clapton was the FENDER; Allman was the GIBSON." Sheesh. I thought Caroline could maybe become my first girlfriend, but her ignorance of the important things in life might be too big an obstacle to overcome.

When Caroline asks about the open notebook on the desk, I tell her about the transcribing. Then she sits down on the floor with my albums and asks if I have any Laura Nyro.

"You should listen to *Eli and the Thirteenth Confession.* You'll recognize a lot of the songs. My sister almost wore her copy straight through."

She finds the album and takes it out of the cover. "What's that smell?"

"Nyro begged the record company to let her have perfumed liner notes. The album's a few years old, but you can still smell it."

Caroline presses the album liner to her face and inhales. I roll my eyes and tell her the songs are good too.

Last time I tried to expand my conversational skills

with Caroline, I ended up making her cry. But I've thought about her brother's bad luck several times since she told me, so I ask how he's doing. It doesn't take long for me to realize I might have made the same mistake again.

"He doesn't want to go to war," she finally says. "My father's really mad. It's been a nightmare. My mother's afraid Billy's going to run away to Canada."

It's probably not the best time to reach for another brownie, but that's what I do.

Caroline stares at me blankly then puts on the happy face she wears at school.

"No, I want to hear more," I say through a mouth of chocolate. "Tell me everything."

She shakes her head and tells me it'll all work out. I feel like a moron letting my sweet tooth get in the way of being there for a potential girlfriend, even one whose musical knowledge is woefully incomplete to make her qualify as one.

When we hear a screech outside, I'm secretly relieved. As the familiar dune buggy zooms into the driveway, I tell Caroline it's my mother and one of her friends.

"I *love* your mom."

"You're going to love her friend too." I don't tell Caroline that when Mom was growing up in Baltimore, one of her family's friends was a little girl named Ellen Naomi Cohen. Little did Mom know as she helped put on plays in the backyard that Ellen would grow up to have an incredible voice, a soaring alto that would rocket the Mamas and the Papas to fame. Now almost everyone calls her Cass Elliot or Mama Cass, but my mother still calls her Ellen. Cass and my mother pretty much run the Canyon scene, which is great for hearing demo tapes and sitting backstage for concerts but not so good for things like clean clothes or prepared dinners. Not that I'm complaining—even with my appetite, I'd take a Ry Cooder session tape over a cheeseburger anytime.

"Quinn! I'm home!" When my mother and Cass enter the kitchen, it's as if the house has been empty all afternoon just waiting for them to burst inside. Between Cass's weight, my mom's hundred-pound frame, and their Indian caftans, they bustle around the kitchen like a batik Laurel and Hardy.

The look on Caroline's face is one of utter shock. She stammers through an introduction, hiding the Laura Nyro album behind her back as if listening to another artist would be cheating on the entire lineup of the Mamas and Papas.

Cass reaches behind Caroline for the album. "This is one of my favorites. Quinnie, can you put it on?"

Cass and my mom put the groceries away as Cass sings along to the Laura Nyro record. Caroline pulls me into my room.

"You didn't tell me you knew Mama Cass!"

I put my finger to my lips and tell her Cass hates to be called Mama. "I've known her my whole life. My sister used to babysit for her daughter, Owen. She's great—you should talk to her." I pull out one of Cass's solo albums and guide Caroline slowly back to the kitchen. When Cass picks up Caroline's discomfort, she gives her a big smile and points to her album.

"See that pink edging all around the cover? That's bubble gum." Cass tells Caroline how Gary Burden was doing work on her house and after he finished, she told him he'd probably be good at designing album covers too. "He and a bunch of our friends chewed a lot of gum which he rolled with a rolling pin, then laid out in this fancy lace pattern. It looks good, doesn't it?"

This is typical Cass—just by noticing Caroline's camera, her intuition tells her the best way to connect with her is through a photograph. Caroline seems to open up and ask more questions. While she thanks my mom for the earrings, I run to my room, take a folder from my desk, and hand it to Cass.

When Mom looks over my shoulder and asks what it is, I tell her it's a belated birthday present. Cass opens the folder and sees my gift: handwritten sheet music for "California Dreamin'." Cass has distanced herself a little from the Mamas and the Papas since she went solo, but it's still the song that reminds me most of her.

She jumps up from the couch. "You took the time to do this for me? Thank you, Quinn!"

She pulls me in for one of her earth-mother hugs while Mom and Caroline examine the pages.

"You took a lot of care with this," Mom says. "It's beautiful."

Caroline also seems impressed. She starts reading the music and singing the familiar song. The rest of us look on in silence; Caroline is as off-key and flat as a singer can possibly be. Really, really BAD. Which for some inexplicable reason makes me like her even more.

When Caroline looks up and sees us, she blushes. "I get carried away sometimes. I'm sure I'm not doing the song justice."

Cass sits back down next to Caroline. "Nonsense—never apologize for singing." She holds up the handwritten sheet music and continues where Caroline left off. They finish the song, Cass's perfect pitch alongside Caroline's flat harmonies. When they're done, my mother gives me a wink and the two of us applaud. Caroline is beaming.

My mother and Cass settle onto the porch with wine and cheese. Caroline runs to the other side of the house and returns with the brownies, an instant hit. She even gets up the nerve to ask if she can take a photo; my mom and Cass happily oblige. I grab us two cans of orange soda from the fridge and we head back to my room, where Caroline helps put my albums back. Somewhere between the C's and D's, our hands accidentally touch. Caroline gives my hand a squeeze.

"Thanks so much for today," she says. "It took my mind off all the stuff going on at home."

She closes her eyes and takes a deep inhale of the Laura Nyro liner notes one more time. It's the perfect moment to reach over and kiss her, so I do. When she pulls her head back to look at me, her look is not of displeasure but surprise.

"Is that okay?" I ask.

"Yeah, fine," Caroline says. "I just didn't expect it, that's all."

My mind immediately goes into overdrive: *I did it wrong. I should've asked. Most guys know what to do—what is wrong with me? Does she hate me now? How are you supposed to know when to try?* The loop of doubt plays over and over like a broken reel-to-reel until Caroline reaches over and kisses me again. I'm just as surprised as she was a moment ago, but unlike her, I don't pull away.

When we finally part, I can taste the orange Fanta of her lips on mine. She brushes her hair behind her ear and tells me she'll see me tomorrow at school. I take a sip of the orange soda, which I'll never be able to drink again without being reminded of this day. I don't give a second thought to Caroline's lack of musical knowledge. Duane Allman—what instrument does he play again?

Caroline waves goodbye to Mom and Cass and when she runs down the driveway, her feet barely touch the ground.

Does this mean I have a girlfriend?

As much as my mind replays that first kiss a hundred times, I also can't stop thinking about how clueless I was when Caroline was talking about her brother. What is my problem? I spend half my time listening to music—is it that much harder to listen to a real person sitting in front of me? If you're thinking Caroline's too good for me, you may be right.

FOR WHAT IT'S WORTH

11/71

Everybody talks about Cass Elliot's voice, but she's also amazing at fixing people up--not in a romantic way, but musically. She knew Graham Nash from the Hollies and when he was in L.A., she told him he had to meet Stephen Stills and David Crosby. She also told him that he should leave the Hollies and sing with them instead. The first time they sang together--in Joni

Mitchell's living room--they harmonized on "You Don't Have to Cry" and immediately knew they had to start a band. CSN never would've happened without Cass.

Love Songs I Can Now Legitimately Sing

★ "Two of Us"—The Beatles

★ "I Got You Babe"—Sonny & Cher

★ "I Want You"—The Beatles

★ "Wouldn't It Be Nice"—The Beach Boys

★ "You Really Got Me"—The Kinks

★ "Love Has Brought Me Around"—James Taylor

★ "Be My Baby"—The Ronettes

★ "Crazy Love"—Van Morrison

★ "All You Need Is Love"—The Beatles

★ "Never Ending Song of Love"—Delaney & Bonnie and Friends

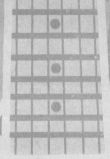

★ **"You've Really Got a Hold on Me"**—
Smokey Robinson & the Miracles

★ **"Hello, I Love You"**—The Doors

★ **"Happy Together"**—The Turtles (Yes, the
song's a little bouncy, a little too happy, but I dare
you to turn it off when it comes on the radio, dare
you not to sing along with the chorus. Besides,
the two lead singers—Mark Volman and Howard
Kaylan, high school friends who grew up near the
airport—ended up joining Zappa's band. And you
can't get any more credible in the rock world than
that.)

I DO have a girlfriend! The next weeks fly by in a flurry of phone calls, lingering at lockers, lots of making out, and MUSIC. I continually add to my list of sappy, embarrassing songs, which now run through my head in a lovestruck loop all day. "Joy to the World," "If You Really Love Me," even super-lame songs like "Colour My World," "Make It With You," and "Sweet Caroline."

Not only am I singing along to the radio to dopey songs by Neil Diamond, I'm singing along with Caroline and her terrible, horrible voice, which doesn't even cause me to wince. Needless to say, Willy and Ryan are horrified by the degradation of my musical taste, but I don't care one bit. It's amazing how a girl I barely knew two months ago has completely shifted my life from idling in neutral to pedal-to-the-metal INCREDIBLE. Caroline walks to school with me, and it's not even weird when Ryan joins us. I try to learn from my mistakes and ask about her brother, how her father likes his new position. Between the store and the Canyon scene, my mother isn't around much, but when she is she gushes about Caroline and sets new pieces of clothing aside for her. (Is she using Caroline as some kind of Soosie replacement? Don't ask me; ask her analyst.)

I'm already in a great mood when I get home from school, but my father raises my spirits even higher by asking if I want to go look at guitars. For some reason, he uses his Ed Sullivan voice which is so bad it makes me cringe—there is absolutely nothing worse than Dad trying to be funny. But since he's taking me to the Guitar Center, I laugh as if he's the next Rich Little.

The Guitar Center is one of my favorite places on the Strip and Dad knows it. He loves to go there too, except he plays around with the amps and soundboards while I drool over the guitars. I don't let myself ask what's prompting Dad's afternoon off; I'm just happy to go along for the ride. I could almost get used to this semi only-child business. I decide today is the day Willy, Ryan, and I go from dreaming about being in the music business to actually trying to break into it. I grab the papers I've been working on all week and hop into the car.

Since I was here last, they've gotten several new

models, including a 1960s Gibson Les Paul that Clapton played in Cream. Before I had a girlfriend, I never would've gotten up the nerve to ask the salesperson to take it down, but I do, even playing a few chords before the clerk demands it back.

When I look over at Dad, he's motioning with his head in that *look who's over there* mode that everyone does when they spot an actor or rock star here. The only person I see is an old black guy with a scarf tied around his head. He's sitting in the corner hunched over an electric slide guitar.

My father pulls me aside. "That's Muddy Waters—the king of Chicago Blues. There wouldn't be any rock and roll if it weren't for guys like him."

Dad doesn't have to explain who Muddy Waters is; anyone who loves rock and roll as much as I do knows how influential he is, especially to so many British bands.

"That Led Zeppelin you love so much ripped Muddy off plenty of times," Dad continues. " 'Whole Lotta Love' is stolen straight from 'You Need Love.' Willie Dixon, who wrote it, should sue."

For the first time, I realize my hyper-knowledge of music might be genetic.

"They stole another Dixon song—'Bring It on Home.' They turned Howlin' Wolf's 'Killing Floor' into 'The Lemon Song.' " What impresses me more than my father's knowledge of musical plagiarism is that he's obviously been dipping into my Zeppelin when I'm not around.

"I'm going to ask him about those twenty-watt tube amps he used to use," Dad says. "He was way ahead of Fender's Super Reverb." He continues listening to the famous bluesman while I complete the most important part of my mission today.

Like many music and record stores, the entrance of the Guitar Center is filled with acres of flyers advertising everything from SINGER WANTED to SPEAKERS FOR SALE. I find a lonely thumbtack and grab the first flyer from my pack.

3 LOCAL KIDS LOOKING FOR
BASS PLAYER TO PRACTICE,
SCORE GIGS, AND MAKE MUSIC!
CONTACT QUINN
555-5895

I stand back and admire my handiwork—a combination of Magic Marker and paisley doodles. I can't wait to tell Willy and Ryan we're finally on our way and can spend some time practicing instead of just coming up with names. (Lemonade Assassins? Analog Sneakers? The list is endless.)

But more than attracting girls or having a cool name, I want the FEELING of being in a band. Maybe it's because I'm stuck with Soosie, but I've always thought being in a band would be like having three or four cool brothers to assist you on your journey to MAKE MUSIC. As I stare up at the flyer, my mind races with the possibility of forming the next Beatles or Rolling Stones. Okay, I might be placing the bar a bit high but it's okay to dream, right?

I hang up the next sign with the same amount of optimism.

MUSIC TRANSCRIPTION

NEAT AND ACCURATE TRANSCRIPTION

OF YOUR ORIGINAL MUSIC.

GOOD PRICES, FAST SERVICE

CONTACT QUINN

555-5895

Getting hired to copy someone's compositions note by note may not sound as cool as starting a band, but I'm just as excited about this job too. Collecting records is EXPENSIVE; I've almost blown through my uncle John's generous birthday cash, as well as my earnings from helping Dad inventory auto parts. Not to mention suddenly having a girlfriend. I need to make some money, pronto.

When I'm finally ready to leave, it takes me several minutes to find my father. He's leaning against the counter with the owner who's sharing his plans to open a store in San Francisco. I can't wait to tell Ryan, whose favorite pastime is to pit San Francisco against L.A. in a musical version of Rock 'Em Sock 'Em Robots. The Dead versus CSN&Y? Jefferson Airplane versus the Mothers of Invention? I also have to tell him step one in the quest for rock-and-roll stardom is completed. On the drive home, we hear "What Is Life?" by George Harrison—his first effort post-Beatles and the first triple album by a solo artist ever. You want to know what life is, George? Life is good. I crank the song up LOUD.

ere's the difference between a normal Guitar Center visit and one when you have a girlfriend: I spend the next hour on the phone with Caroline in the kitchen eating peanuts and rehashing the afternoon. It's as if every life event gets multiplied by two—when I first experience it, then again when I share it with her. No one told me having a girlfriend increases every other aspect of your life exponentially.

FOR WHAT IT'S WORTH

11/71

Jefferson Airplane is the only band to
play all three famous rock-and-roll
concerts: Woodstock, Monterey Pop, and
Altamont. The last one is infamous,
more for the offstage events than the
onstage: there were three accidental
deaths and one homicide. The Rolling
Stones hired the Hells Angels to be in
charge of security--kind of like hiring
a group of foxes on motorcycles to

guard the henhouse--and they bullied
the unruly crowd so much that Jagger
had to constantly beg the audience to
be cool. When a wasted eighteen-year-
old charged the stage with a gun, one
of the Hells Angels fatally stabbed him
right there in front of everyone. He
later was found not guilty, but the
incident marked a real turning point
for the whole "peace and love"
Woodstock Nation. The concert is
captured in the documentary Gimme
Shelter, killing and all.

The calls start coming, and within a few weeks, Ryan, Willy, and I have set up five auditions for a bass player. We're starting a band! When I ask if it's okay to bring Caroline along to Willy's house, I worry he and Ryan will go all Yoko on me, but both of them say it's okay. I'm not saying this just because she's my girl-friend, but for someone who was living three thousand miles away a few months ago, Caroline seems to have adjusted well. She's good friends with a few of the girls in our class, boys too. She shoots photos for the school paper and has even snuck into a few clubs with Ashley without using Soosie's name. It's pretty much only her rapid-fire East Coast speech pattern that tips you off that she's not a born and bred Angeleno.

The first kid doesn't show up for the audition, but the

second guy comes half an hour early so it evens out. He's sixteen and says he's been playing since he was twelve. He must've been playing something besides bass, because his version of Van Morrison's "Wild Night" is the worst I've ever heard.

I keep checking in with Caroline, but she waves me off like she's fine and doesn't need babysitting. SEE WHAT A COOL GIRLFRIEND I HAVE?

The next guy, Marvin, is from Inglewood. He plugs his Fender in and wails on Alice Cooper's "Under My Wheels." I love the song anyway but didn't realize how much it needed a bass when we usually practice it. (It needs horns too, but that's not going to happen anytime soon.) Willy thinks we should offer Marvin the gig right away, but Ryan and I agree it's only fair to audition the other candidates coming later. Marvin packs up his bass and heads back down the Canyon to catch a bus back home.

"He was good," Caroline says when he leaves. "I bet he's the best one you see."

"Yeah, plus, he seems like a good guy, which is just as important as his guitar skills." I look over to see Willy and Ryan checking out the two of us and I'm transported to the first day of school when they goofed on me for approaching Caroline. Ryan's gone out with three girls since then, but I'm happy to finally be with just one.

The four of us split a pizza and two bags of potato

chips before the next person shows up. He's twelve years old and a disaster. The only reason we don't kick him out halfway through the first song is that he reminds Caroline of a kid she used to babysit for and she gives us the evil eye to be nice to him or else. Next is a fifteen-year-old who plays really well—great, in fact—but she's got this snotty Bel Air attitude none of us can stomach, so we send her on her way. In the end, we decide Marvin is the best fit for the band and call to let him know.

On the way home, Caroline, Ryan, and I feverishly dissect the lyrics of "American Pie." Ryan and I argue that "the day the music died" refers to the plane crash that killed Richie Valens, Buddy Holly, and the Big Bopper, but Caroline cites the "Father, Son, and Holy Ghost" line as evidence of a religious theme. We argue all the way back up Lookout Mountain, collapsing with laughter in front of Caroline's house. It's not just deconstructing the song that has us so giddy—Ryan and I have just taken the first step in our musical careers and our energy can't be contained. And Caroline's our first fan, maybe even groupie. As we lie on the lawn of thyme, it occurs to me that my life may never be this great again. It's sappy perfect—Phil Spector–produced perfect—and I immediately feel my body clench. If things are this good, something bad inevitably has to happen soon. But nothing terrible happens; Caroline kisses me goodbye and gives Ryan a good-natured hug too.

"Remember her on the first day of school?" Ryan asks.

"I was just thinking about that."

"She's almost hot now."

I punch him in the arm but am secretly flattered.

I get home just in time for Dad to put a plate of tacos on the table. I'm not one to complain about any kind of Mexican food, but it's the third time this week Mom's missed dinner and we've had takeout. I pick at the chunks of avocado, gathering my thoughts before speaking. (This might be a first.)

"Is Mom okay? Is she still upset Soosie's not coming home for the holidays?"

When my father looks at the window before answering, it seems as if he's trying to transport himself somewhere else. (PS—Speaking of teleportation, why did they cancel *Star Trek*? Enough with the repeats—we need new episodes!)

"It has nothing to do with Soosie," he finally answers. "Her priorities are a little messed up right now, that's all."

"You mean like . . . partying?"

"A bit too much, yes." My father has never liked going to parties or having them, as opposed to Mom, who takes full advantage of the nonstop Canyon social scene without him. He points to the two tacos still left on the plate. "We'll save these for her."

I retract my hand, which was about to grab one of the tacos, and get out the plastic wrap instead. I leverage Dad's concern about Mom by asking if I can stay up to watch *Night Gallery*. Both he and Mom are pretty insistent about me going to bed on time but tonight he lets me stay up. He wonders if the show is too creepy to watch before bed, but I remind him Soosie's the family scaredy-cat, not me. Tonight's episode is a repeat of the pilot, which is still my favorite. It ends badly—as most of these do—with a *Twilight Zone* twist that has my father pounding his hand on the armchair in satisfaction. As I round up the glasses from the coffee table to place in the sink, I casually ask Dad if he wants me to wait up with him.

"No, no. Off to bed with you." He uses his Rod Serling voice, which is one of the only impersonations he's actually good at.

I head to my room and hope Mom's on her way home or at least finds a phone to call and relieve Dad's worrying. I didn't call Caroline tonight but will meet her in the morning at the top of the street to walk to school. It's crazy to think my parents have more relationship problems than I do right now.

The creepiness of *Night Gallery* hovers over me as I take out my Ouija board. It's the first time I've used it alone all week; it's actually been much more fun using it with Caroline. I place my fingers on the planchette and ask if my mother's okay. I'm about to read out the letters when I hear a knock on my door.

"Just wanted to say good night," Dad says.

Unlike Mom, Dad doesn't disapprove of my fascination with the supernatural and asks if he can join me.

"Sure." I take a deep breath before continuing. "I was just wondering about Mom."

"Well, let's see what Mr. Ouija has to say." His hands—worn and stained from a decade of fixing engines—seem surprisingly delicate when he rests them on the planchette.

"Is Mom okay?" I ask again.

I spell out the letters as the Ouija marks them. **W-E A-R-E W-O-R-R-I-E-D**.

"We?" I ask. "It's never said that before."

"Must be referring to you and me." He looks up and nods slightly. "It might be time for a family powwow."

I nod in agreement, but all I'm thinking is CAN'T YOU FIX THIS WITHOUT ME—I'm only fourteen! Our brief conversation with the Ouija gods seems to boost Dad's courage, because when he leaves my room, he's determined and confident. My mother—if she were here instead of gallivanting with her friends—would kill us both for playing this game, especially for asking personal questions about her.

I don't say anything to Dad, but I AM worried. You'd have to live under a rock not to know that drugs and alcohol permeate the city as much as creativity does. My mother's always been social—half the reason she loves having the store is that she can talk to people all day—but I'm concerned she might be in over her head. Why am I worried about my mom coming home all hours of the night, anyway? Shouldn't it be the other way around? I wait to hear the screen door open but fall asleep before it does.

I still don't understand the Ouija board saying "we." Just because I'm part of a couple now, the Ouija gods are too?

FOR WHAT IT'S WORTH

11/71

Alice Cooper--real name Vincent
Furnier--is actually a clean-cut
athlete from Phoenix and the son of a
preacher. He and the other guys on his
cross-country team decided to form a
band for the high school talent show.
Vincent loved performing but wanted a
more theatrical moniker; he came up
with Alice Cooper, the name of a
17th-century witch. The band moved to

L.A. with their preppy letterman
sweaters, and it wasn't long before
they were discovered by musical genius
extraordinaire Frank Zappa. Zappa's
protégés, the GTO's, a group of young
party girls from the Valley, used to
dress up Alice and his friends in
their wacky outfits, giving rise to
the shock-horror look they sport today.
And how did Alice find out about a
17th-century witch? Believe it or not,
a Ouija board.

Turns out Mom was at a late-night recording session at Cass's house and got home after I fell asleep. At breakfast the next morning, she seems perfectly normal, frying eggs while jotting notes in her dream journal. I wait for Dad to call the dreaded powwow but am grateful to be spared. We have a low-key Thanksgiving with take-out from Barney's and a hike in Fryman Canyon. I spend the rest of the weekend trying to figure out what to get Caroline for Christmas. (A pendant made from the plastic inserts for my 45s?) The rest of the time goes to wearing out *Led Zeppelin IV*, which Jeff at the record store turned me on to last month.

Two of the songs are over seven minutes; one of them—"Stairway to Heaven"—is just over eight, almost a minute longer than "Hey Jude." The bass and drums don't even kick in until the song's half over. Willy says the words don't make any sense, but I don't care. (As if anyone understands the lyrics of "Immigrant Song.") After the conversation with Dad at the Guitar Center regarding Zeppelin's musical ethics, I can't help thinking that the opening guitar arpeggios of "Stairway" are *very* reminiscent of Randy California's guitar work on Spirit's "Taurus," an instrumental. The fact that Zeppelin opened for Spirit a few years ago makes me wonder about the "coincidence" even more. But there's no denying Page's skill. The guitar solo is so amazing it makes me want to give up playing because I'll never be as good as he is. It also makes me want to practice ten hours a day to try.

I decide to walk over and see if Caroline wants to give it yet another listen. On the way over, I run into Sonya at the Canyon Store. She's been in my class since sixth grade and is the only person I know who wears contact lenses—these hard disks you actually put in your eyes. The whole thing sounds scary, but I have to admit Sonya looks great without her wire glasses. We talk about Mr. Woodrow, our latest substitute teacher, and how he's giving us too much homework. I hang out with her for a while before heading up the hill to Caroline's house.

Caroline's mother waves me through the sunny kitchen. She's on the phone, slicing a mound of mushrooms on the wooden counter. Between the embroidered

dress she got at my mom's store and the bucolic sur-
roundings, she should be the picture of happiness. But
she looks tired, and I wonder if she's still worried about
Caroline's brother in boot camp. I look around the kitchen
for any sign of Caroline and finally spot her outside.

With Ryan.

"What are you guys doing?" I ask.

"High-low-jack," Caroline says. "Want to play?"

"I mean why are you hanging out—without me?"

Ryan pretends to rearrange his cards and barely
looks up.

Caroline jumps out of her chair. "We ran into each
other at the store and I invited Ryan over. What's the big
deal?"

"No big deal," I backpedal. "I was just at the store
too—with Sonya. Thought I'd stop by since I was already
out." I feel bad for name-dropping a pretty girl in our
class but not THAT bad.

"I've invited Sonya over twice," Caroline says. "I
don't think she likes me."

Ryan finally decides to speak. "Don't take it personally. Sonya can be a real snob."

As if Ryan is the expert on every girl in our class.

Ryan—who I just started a band with.

Ryan—who's had girls hanging all over him since
kindergarten.

Ryan—who has a black bedroom!

Caroline shuffles the deck and starts to deal me in, but I tell her I have to go. Almost embarrassed, I wave the new album in the air. "Just thought you might want to hear this again."

"You're so funny," she says. "You're obsessed with that album."

Ryan throws in his two cents. "It's okay."

When Caroline's mother calls her inside, I plop on the chair next to Ryan. "*Zeppelin IV* is OKAY? Are you kidding?"

"Look, don't make a big deal out of me being here. Caroline's *your* girlfriend—you of all people know how friendly she is. She invited me over and I said yes."

My mind tries to make sense of the situation. Does Caroline already have one foot out the door?

Caroline returns and pulls out all the stops—the tilted head, the scrunched-up nose. "Ryan brought over *American Beauty.* Do you want to hear it?"

"You mean MY *American Beauty*?" What is going on with my best friend?

"Mine was at my father's—I just got it back. Here." He tosses me the album as if it's a Frisbee, and I have to dive across the chair to catch it. I can't get out of here fast enough, and tell them I have to go.

Caroline practically runs down the driveway after me. "Are you mad? We were just hanging out."

I hold up the album like a visor to block the sun. "It's

not a problem. I'll talk to you tonight." When I look back at Ryan, he waves goodbye over his head without glancing up from his cards. Did I miss something? I walked home from school with him today. We talked about how well Marvin is doing in the band; he didn't mention anything about Caroline. I guess since she traded in wool skirts for bell-bottoms, he's changed his mind about her. And what about Caroline wearing earrings I gave her—okay, technically they're from my mom—while she lounges in the yard with Ryan? Or am I the problem, especially in these open-door, open-minded times? Maybe nothing is going on at all and I'm being ridiculous.

Back at my house, I drag out the Ouija board. I check the other rooms to make sure my mother's not home.

"What's wrong with me?" I ask. "What's going on?"

Both questions are too vague to play the game properly, but the planchette starts to move anyway. I have to scramble to remember all the letters but I do. **W-E T-H-I-N-K Y-O-U-R-E L-O-S-I-N-G H-E-R**.

As soon as I realize what the letters spell, the opening riff to Rod Stewart's "(I Know) I'm Losing You" fills my head. I flip through my albums, find *Every Picture Tells a Story*, and put it on the turntable. Is the Ouija right? Am I losing Caroline? Is it a hard-and-fast rule that being in a group means losing your girlfriend to one of your bandmates? Are we already playing out a Brian Jones/Anita Pallenberg/Keith Richards love triangle? We haven't even had a gig yet! Since no one's home, I crank the song up loud, wallowing in the fact that my best friend is no longer acting like my best friend. Or am I just overanalyzing again?

It might sound crazy, but I still can't get over the Ouija using the word *we*. I remember other kids talking about the different voices and personalities their Ouija boards picked up—like changing channels on the radio. Just last year, one of Soosie's friends swore she channeled some crazy demon from Scandinavia.

When the song's done, I lower the volume and ask the Ouija another question. "Who are you?" As the Ouija responds, I say the letters out loud in an attempt to remember them all.

J·I·M·I J·A·N·I·S J·I·M.

My hand jumps off the planchette as if it's on fire. My mother has always insisted that the Ouija isn't a game, that evil spirits can find their way into the innocent questions people ask. Jimi, Janis, Jim? I've either tapped into a group of people whose names begin with the letter *J* or I've stumbled into the underground world of Club 27.

I know what you're thinking—why are some of the biggest names in rock-and-roll history offering advice to a scrawny kid from Bancroft Junior High?

THAT'S WHAT I WANT TO KNOW.

This whole thing scares the snot out of me, yet I have to admit I'm intrigued. Is this some kind of hoax or is it real? And how can I tell the difference?

FOR WHAT IT'S WORTH

11/71

Jimmy Page often uses a violin bow to play his Fender Telecaster and Les Paul guitars. He learned the trick from another session musician, David McCallum, Sr.--a member of the Royal Philharmonic who played on one of my favorite Beatles songs, "A Day in the Life." McCallum's son plays Russian secret agent Illya Kuryakin on The Man from U.N.C.L.E., a show I never miss in reruns. The father of a Scottish actor who plays a Russian spy teaches musical innovations to a British guitar god-- why isn't my life full of random connections like that?

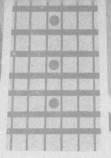

Songs About Ghosts and Death

★ "All Things Must Pass"—George Harrison

★ "Spirit in the Sky"—Norman Greenbaum

★ "Black Sabbath"—Black Sabbath

★ "Wicked Annabella"—The Kinks

★ "Gallows Pole"—Led Zeppelin

★ "Black Magic Woman"—Santana

★ "Sympathy for the Devil"—The Rolling Stones

★ "Spooky"—Classics IV

★ "Battle of Evermore"—Led Zeppelin

★ "Break on Through to the Other Side"—The Doors

★ "A Day in the Life"—The Beatles

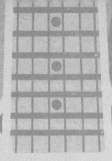

★ **"Children of the Grave"**—Black Sabbath

★ **"Something in the Air"**—Thunderclap Newman, a one-hit wonder band created by Pete Townshend for his longtime chauffeur and roadie, Speedy Keen. The group disbanded soon after, but I still love this song.

I can tell by Caroline's expression she's come over to apologize. (That and the conciliatory plate of still-warm peanut butter cookies.) Betty Crocker offering or not, I'm still pretty bummed out.

"I ran into Ryan at the store," she begins. "He's in your band—I was being nice."

The fact that she says MY band helps me take a mini step in forgiving her.

"We were just playing cards. You should've stayed."

My voice sounds pathetic and vulnerable even to me. "But why didn't you call me?"

"My mother was on the phone! I asked her ten times to get off, but she wouldn't."

I have to admit that part of the story is undeniably true.

"She's so upset about my brother—she calls him all the time."

Her logical argument and cookie #2 go a long way to assuage my anger. I pull Caroline toward me, and all is right with the world.

"Besides," she says. "I know Ryan's your best friend, but he's so in love with himself."

Bashing Ryan's eternal confidence locks in 100 percent of my forgiveness. I decide to tell Caroline about my secret new discovery, but NOT what Club 27 said about losing her.

She bursts into laughter when I explain the ghosts now inhabiting my Ouija board. "Club 27! That can't possibly be true."

I lead her by the hand to find out for herself.

"I don't trust you with this thing. Besides, you know too much about music—you could skew every answer."

I'm insulted by her lack of trust. Yes, I know, another double standard after I just accused her of fooling around with my best friend. Cheating at Ouija would be just as wrong, believe me.

"Okay," she says. "But *I'll* ask the questions."

As happy as I am to share this crazy find with Caroline, I'm just as thrilled that we've so easily overcome our first relationship hurdle. Just for good measure, I initiate a quick make-out session. After a while, she laughs and pushes me away. "You're keeping me from Club 27. Come on!"

Out of all the questions you could ask the notorious singer who changed the way white women sang the blues, Caroline asks who took the photograph on the front cover of *Pearl*. Really? That's what you want to ask Janis Joplin? I lower my head as the planchette begins to move so Caroline doesn't see me smile.

"B-A-R-R-Y," Caroline reads aloud.

I stare at the letters in disbelief, then rush to my albums and flip through the *J*'s until I find *Pearl* and scan the liner notes.

"Barry Feinstein," I read. "I wouldn't have known that with a gun to my head."

Caroline's eyes shine like a toddler on her first pony ride. "Let's do it again."

Her next question also refers to an album cover—she asks who drew the cartoons on *Cheap Thrills*.

"C-R-U-M-B." She looks across the board at me, our faces just inches apart. "What does *that* mean?"

This time I DO know the answer. "R. Crumb. He's an underground comic artist—his stuff is wild." I pull out the album and show it to her.

"Do you want to ask anything about music?" I ask. "Or talk to Jim or Jimi?"

"Are you kidding? I want to go home and call half the kids in our class."

I have no idea what she's talking about.

"This is a gold mine! We have to line up customers, start charging for this."

This new side to my girlfriend is intriguing and a little devious.

"Back in Hartford, my friend Kim and I used to come up with different ways to make money. I took pictures of people's kids, then she made collages, we tie-dyed T-shirts, organized birthday parties—all kinds of things. Our friends will pay to talk to Janis, Jimi, and Jim, don't you think?"

As much as I'm always scrounging around the neighborhood for odd jobs to earn extra money, I never once thought of this portal to Club 27 as a means to extra cash. But if some kid in my class said HE was talking to Hendrix, you better believe I'd be first in line to check it out.

"Okay," I finally answer. "But you're in charge of bringing people in. We split the proceeds fifty-fifty."

"Call me tonight and we'll put together our plan."

Sure, I'm excited about a new idea to improve my cash flow—TRANSLATION: BUY MORE ALBUMS—but what I focus on now are Caroline's pronouns. WE have to line up customers. OUR plan. The relationship seems firmly back on track. I pour myself a celebratory glass of milk to go along with cookie #3 and grab the phone on the first ring.

"Is this Quinn?" a low voice asks. I take a huge

swallow before answering, but the voice doesn't wait. "I saw your sign at the Guitar Center. You transcribe music?"

I'd almost forgotten about the other ad that I posted several weeks ago.

"How about if I give you a piece to try? What do you charge?"

It's a question I haven't given any thought to and blurt out the first number that comes to mind. "Ten dollars?"

"You sure that's not too much?"

"Eight?"

"I'm just kidding. Ten is fine."

I tell him I live in the Canyon and he asks me to meet him in the parking lot of the store in ten minutes. An actual paying job! Between this and Caroline's new Ouija idea, I'm suddenly golden.

I skid my bike into the dusty parking lot of the Canyon Store and wait for my new employer to arrive. I try not to be nervous but can't help it—this is my first professional job in the music business. Sure, I've transcribed pieces for Cass for fun, but never as a real gig.

When a guy with curly dark hair, skinny striped bell-bottoms, and a long mustache walks toward me, my bike falls out of my hand and clatters to the pavement.

"You must be Quinn," the man says. "I'm Frank Zappa."

Okay, you have to understand what it means to meet this guy in person. I LOVE Zappa, have every Mothers of Invention LP, as well as every solo album. I have records he just produced, like Captain Beefheart's *Trout Mask Replica*. (On the list of the top ten best album covers EVER.) Zappa's "Peaches en Regalia" on *Hot Rats* is my #1 instrumental OF ALL TIME, and is even in the top ten of my list of desert island songs—an instrumental—THAT'S how good it is. I've seen Frank and his crazy entourage around the Canyon but have never spoken to him face-to-face. Transcribing his complicated, unwieldy, beautiful music note by note is something I'd do for free.

FOR WHAT IT'S WORTH

12/71

Frank Zappa's father was a chemist who worked at several chemical plants. Because of nearby mustard gas arsenals, Frank grew up with gas masks all around the house. He started playing with sound at an early age, began composing orchestral pieces in high school, even conducting the school band in one of his original arrangements. For his 15th birthday, he asked to make a long-distance phone call to the French composer Edgard Varèse. When he was 22, he went on The Steve Allen Show playing a bicycle with drumsticks and a bow. The musicians in his band were shocked to discover he expected them

each to read and play his sheet music note for note, an unusual practice in rock and roll. His songs are full of dark humor, as are his album covers. We're Only in It for the Money features Frank and the Mothers of Invention in a parody of the Beatles' Sergeant Pepper.

Mr. Woodrow is trying way too hard to be voted most popular substitute teacher. He hurries us through the section on figures of speech, then gets to what he REALLY wants to talk about today: Simon and Garfunkel's *Bridge over Troubled Water*. It's a record I liked until Soosie played it nonstop when it came out last year. After a few months, I wanted to send the disk hurling out the window.

"Paul Simon is a poet," Mr. Woodrow begins. "Let's listen to a few of these songs, then discuss the lyrics." He goes to the closet in the back of the room and brings the battered turntable to his desk.

I'm all for listening to music in class—especially if it'll get us out of talking about similes and metaphors—but somehow analyzing a song's lyrics with a teacher takes the fun out of listening. When Simon wrote *sail on, silver girl,* who was he referring to—a woman he knew? These are the kind of questions I might ask myself as I lie on the floor of my room with my headphones on, but it feels almost blasphemous to be talking about them in class with a guy whose pants are pulled up to his armpits. Private, personal—both for Paul Simon and for me. I spend most of the class slouching lower in my seat so Mr. Woodrow doesn't call on me.

Caroline raises her hand. "The song's about comforting someone in need, a friend."

Ryan's hand shoots up right behind her. "It's dramatic, building up to a big finale."

The thing is, Ryan HATES this song, used to call it "Bilge over Dirty Water" whenever Soosie had it on. The fact that he's using it as a way to suck up to Caroline makes me raise my hand too.

"It's one of the only songs that Garfunkel sang alone," I continue. "Simon really regretted it. It was a monster hit, but they broke up right after." I could tell Woodrow lots of other info about the song—that the engineer got that drum sound in the middle by placing a snare at the bottom of an elevator shaft and miking it from above—but I've succeeded in my mission, switching Caroline's attention from Ryan to me.

I take it in stride when Caroline loops her arm through mine in the hall. "You know so much about music," she says. "Let me help you with one of your columns so I can learn."

All I can think about is what a mess *Two Virgins* was when John and Yoko tried to collaborate.

"I know it's your thing," Caroline says. "I'm not trying to interfere. I just thought it would be cool to do something together. But if you don't want to, we can just concentrate on the Ouija business."

"No, let's do it over break. It'll be fun."

"Hey, I saw you on your porch last night," she continues. "You were with your Dad—I didn't want to disturb you."

"What were you doing out so late?"

She shrugs as if the answer is not important, but inside I'm screaming, WERE YOU WITH RYAN AGAIN?

Caroline unfastens herself from my arm to catch up with Lindy and Willy, leaving me enveloped by my imagination's worst-case scenarios. *I thought we were good? I thought you wanted to do a column together?*

As I meet Ryan outside school to walk home, I decide not to ask him about his plans last night. But I can't resist busting his chops about English class. "For somebody who doesn't like Simon and Garfunkel, you had a lot to say today."

"I've got a C in that class. I figure it's easier to participate in a discussion about music than talking about stupid spoonerisms, whatever they are." He changes the subject by making me tell him yet again about my meeting with Zappa.

What I REALLY need is to talk to him about my conversation with his idol, the Lizard King. It may sound petty, but I've been holding back telling Ryan about Club 27 and my Ouija board as a way to punish him for that day at Caroline's. But he's so happy about my encounter with Zappa that I feel guilty, so as we walk I decide to tell him. He stops in his tracks about halfway through the story.

"Let me get this straight"—he laughs—"Jim Morrison, the lead singer of the Doors, talks to you through your Ouija board?"

"Along with Janis Joplin and Jimi Hendrix—I know it sounds ridiculous, but it's true. I was asking Hendrix guitar tips all night."

"First you think I'm stealing your girlfriend, now this? You're losing it, Quinn."

"Come on, I'll show you. Ask him anything you want."

"Uhm, thanks but no thanks."

The fact that he doesn't even consider the possibility of such a thing angers me almost as much as discovering him at Caroline's.

"Why would I make this up?" I ask.

"My question exactly." He punches me on the arm good-naturedly, as if the whole conversation isn't worth further discussion. "My dad picked up tickets to tonight's Lakers game. Wilt's on fire—I can't wait."

Ryan obviously isn't interested in the intricacies of Club 27, so I follow along and talk about the Lakers. It's hard not to be envious of how this whole divorce thing has been a giant boon for Ryan. My mother read some article about how parents separating can be hard on the kids, but Ryan's mom and dad are so busy taking him to games and concerts, buying him new clothes and albums, he hasn't had time to feel sad. It almost makes me wish my parents would start fighting more.

I tell him I'll meet him at Willy's for practice later and he climbs the fence for the shortcut back to his house. As I walk up the hill on my own, though, I get a strange feeling someone is following me. Maybe all this talk about Ouija spirits is seeping into my brain. I decide to put an end to this creepy nonsense and whip around to see if anyone's behind me. I nearly jump into the air like a cartoon character when someone is following me, a guy who also walked behind me on the way to school this morning.

"What's your problem?" I ask. "What do you want?"

He seems to be about eighteen or nineteen, with dirty jeans and a new beard. He looks as if he hasn't slept in days.

"I'm a friend of your sister's," he says. "I worked at Brandeis and we hung out a lot."

"You know Soosie?"

He stops and holds out his hand. "My name's Brett.

Your sister told me if I got into a jam, I should contact you."

"Me? I'm only fourteen. I don't even have my driver's license." I stop too, trying to process this new information. "You're in a jam? What did you do?"

Brett sits down on the bench outside the store. He looks around to make sure no one's listening before he answers. "I didn't show up to the draft board. There's a warrant out for my arrest. I'm looking at serious jail time."

This must be Soosie's friend from the deli. What's he doing here following ME?

"I'm deciding if I should go to Canada," he says. "I'll probably only be here for a few weeks, but if you have any food to spare, I'd sure appreciate it. I ran out of money back in Arizona."

I ask him where he's staying and am shocked when he tells me the woods.

"There are coyotes, even mountain lions," I say. "Why don't you come to our house?"

He shakes his head. "I'm wanted by the law. I don't want to get anybody in trouble." He gets up and stretches when a mother with two kids walks by. "Any leftovers you can get your hands on would be great. I've never been a fussy eater and I'm not about to start now."

When he gives me a crooked smile, it suddenly dawns

on me that this guy hasn't given me one shred of proof that he knows Soosie. He could be a vagrant who's never met my sister. I imagine my mother's spiel about how close we came to having one of Manson's family stay with us a few years ago.

"Can you prove you know Soosie?"

He smiles again, this time a bit sadly. "She left you a present when she came east. You never found it."

I guess he DOES know her. "Did she tell you what it was?"

"I'll give you a hint," he answers. "Dave Mason." He heads back up toward the dusky canyon. "I'll be a few yards off the trailhead. If you can't help, no problem. It was nice meeting you anyway."

I race back to my room and flip through my records. I check my Traffic albums for any notes—nothing. I find Dave Mason's solo album, *Alone Together*, and start to smile. Soosie's always known how much I covet the marbleized vinyl of her album. I was devastated when I bought one for myself and just got the run-of-the-mill black record, not knowing the funky swirled vinyl she'd bought was a limited first edition. I'd torn my room apart looking for a present, never guessing she'd swapped my album for hers.

I drop the needle onto the disc and watch the colors swirl across the turntable as Mason sings "Only You

Know and I Know." (He did an album with Cass this year; Mom went with her to *The Tonight Show* when they performed from it live.)

The good news is, I now have an album I've lusted after for years. The bad news? I have a fugitive hiding in the woods by my house. I'm not sure about the trade-off.

So what do I do—let the guy starve? At Christmas-time?!

Or do I help a draft dodger hiding from the police?

All I want is to stay in my musical cocoon—is that asking too much?

FOR WHAT IT'S WORTH

1/72

If you do a family tree for British
rock, you see a lot of places where the
branches and roots converge. Eric
Clapton played in the Yardbirds with
Jeff Beck but not at the same time as
Jimmy Page, who went on to form Led
Zeppelin. Clapton, Ginger Baker, and
Jack Bruce formed the influential
supergroup Cream; Clapton and Baker
then joined up with Steve Winwood from

Traffic to form yet another supergroup,
Blind Faith. Winwood used to be in
Traffic with Dave Mason. These bands
were not only known for their music;
they were famous for their album covers
too. Cream's Disraeli Gears is a
psychedlic classic, Blind Faith's only
album freaked people out with its
controversial cover depicting a
shirtless young girl; and everyone
loved Traffic's Low Spark of High
Heeled Boys, with its optical illusion
design and corner cutaways.

I spend most of the holiday break wondering what to do about Brett. I want to help the guy, but I don't want to be arrested. I take a baby step in the crime department and use the whistle to call Soosie at school. She stops me before I start talking and tells me she'll call right back. By the time I make myself a ham sandwich, the phone rings.

"I didn't want to use the dorm phone," she says. "Brett is breaking the law. The authorities are looking for him."

"Why did you tell him about me? What can I do?"

"He didn't know where he was going—cross country, Canada—I told him if he landed in L.A., he could look you up. He's a good guy, Quinn."

I ask why she didn't have him come to the house and ask Mom and Dad for help instead.

"So Dad could talk him into going off to war like he

did?" She sounds exasperated. "If you don't want to help, don't. I just thought you might want to get involved for a change."

"For the millionth time, the war has nothing to do with me!"

"It doesn't have anything to do with Brett either," she says. "Eighteen-year-olds just got the vote six months ago—no one getting drafted has even voted in a presidential election."

I roll my eyes at Soosie's impromptu lecture on the Twenty-sixth Amendment, as if Mr. Woodrow hasn't hit us over the head with it a dozen times already.

Soosie's voice softens. "I forget you're still young and the draft doesn't affect you yet. It'll be a big deal for you in a few years. I hope you never have to find out what Brett's going through."

I'm relieved to be saved from more political discussion when Caroline knocks on the back door wearing the denim skirt I bought her for Christmas at my mother's store. As I say goodbye to Soosie, I decide not to tell Caroline about Brett. It's not that I want to keep secrets from my girlfriend, but I know how hard it is with her brother in Vietnam, and the last thing I want to do is bring up a sore subject. I don't have to worry about it, though, because all Caroline wants to talk about is our column and new business. Who knew my new girlfriend was such a marketing genius?

For the Ouija idea, she's recruited Tom, the biggest Hendrix fan in our class. His guitar skills are well below yours truly, but he has every album Hendrix ever made, including bootlegs. When Hendrix died a few weeks into school last year, Tom didn't show up for three days, missing so much football practice the coach cut him from the team. Now this kid who would never in a million years hang out at my house is walking up my driveway, hands shoved into the pockets of his denim jacket.

We sit on the rug in my bedroom and stare at the Ouija board between us.

"You sure it's Hendrix you're talking to?" Tom asks.

"I can't guarantee it," I say, "but it certainly sounds like him to me."

"You can pay us after if you want," Caroline adds. "We're not trying to rip anybody off."

This seems to placate Tom, who places his beefy fingers on the planchette. I put mine opposite his while Caroline sits on the bed poised to take notes.

"Okay, what do you want to ask Jimi?" Caroline seems to like her role as foreman of the operation.

"I want to ask about 'Foxey Lady,'" Tom says. "How come *foxy* is spelled wrong?"

I lower my head in feigned concentration so Tom can't see me roll my eyes. You can pick the brain of one of the greatest guitarists of our time and you ask about a spelling error? You don't ask why he plays the F-sharp on the second fret with his thumb or how he does that killer 7#9? What is WRONG with you? I don't dare look at Caroline, who gives me a little kick with her clog as if she can read my mind.

As the planchette moves across the board, I say the letters aloud to Caroline, who reads them back to Tom.

"Record company typo," she says.

"It's true," I say. "They spelled it wrong on the U.S. album but correctly on the British."

Tom nods as if we've solved the Riddle of the Sphinx. But just as suddenly his mood shifts. "How do I know you didn't move it?"

" 'Cuz I don't cheat," I answer. "It would be like a band lip-syncing—what's the point?" I tell him to ask something else.

Tom starts to get the hang of it and asks some good questions about "Hey Joe" and Electric Ladyland Studios. By the time the planchette cruises to the GOOD BYE part of the board, Tom can barely contain his grin.

"That was great. Can I come by tonight with Lynne? She worshipped Jimi—Janis too." He jams his hand into his pocket, this time emerging with a five-dollar bill, which I happily relieve him of.

After Tom leaves, Kathye and Paula arrive on their bikes. They pretty much just want to ask Jim Morrison a million questions, none of them having anything to do with his music. Normally their lame *Tiger Beat* questions would infuriate me, but today I ask the Ouija patiently, without a trace of sarcasm or musical snobbery. I look over to Caroline, meticulously taking notes as if the details of Morrison's love life need a dedicated secretary. She tilts her head in that way that just kills me and I'm good for another round of ridiculous Morrison interrogation.

When my mom stops home to change clothes, I'm secretly glad we're between "clients" and the Ouija board is back underneath my bed. My mother wouldn't be happy with me spending so much time in the world of the supernatural and would be even less happy with me making money off my friends. Although to be honest, no one who's taken advantage of our direct portal to Club 27 can technically be categorized as "friend." Most of them barely register on the acquaintance scale.

After my mother leaves, Caroline readies the room for our last visitors, but all I'm thinking about is more making out. The last thing on my mind is channeling Janis Joplin's drunken stories for the entertainment of Tom's girlfriend, but Lynne's questions are thoughtful, without an ounce of the tabloid gossip I braced myself for. As I sit across the board from her in the relaxed concentration the Ouija calls for, it dawns on me that it's almost a double date, that Caroline and I are spending a Friday night with the most popular couple at school. Poor Janis might have been an unpopular, overweight teen with bad skin back in Port Arthur, Texas, but she's helping my popularity climb to the top of the charts today.

Tom pays us the five dollars for Lynne's session. Then I walk them to the door. "Maybe we can all hang out sometime," I suggest. "You can come hear my band."

Tom looks at me as if I've just asked for the recipe for pineapple Bundt cake. Lynne thanks me for the session.

"It was great to talk to Janis again," she adds. "I used to see her outside Barney's Beanery all the time. I really miss her." She tells Tom she'll catch up with him outside, then looks over her shoulder at Caroline back in my room. "If you two are still together, let's all go hear some music."

If we're still together? What's THAT supposed to mean?

The screen door slams between us, and when I turn around, Caroline is standing right behind me.

"Another satisfied customer," she says. "Are you okay?"

"Yeah, just tired."

"You worked hard today." She looks at the kitchen clock and grabs her patchwork bag by the door. "I gotta go or my mom's gonna kill me." She stands across from me, waiting. So I reach across the chasm of newfound doubt and kiss her. She scrunches up her nose and tells me she'll see me at school tomorrow.

I run my tongue across my lips; this time, there's not a trace of Fanta.

Of course I race back to the board to get a read on Lynne's comment.

"Is Caroline going to break up with me?" I ask.

S·H·E I·S U·N·H·A·P·P·Y, the Ouija answers.

"But what did I do?"

This time the question remains unanswered.

FOR WHAT IT'S WORTH

2/72

Usually an original song is hands down better than the cover version, but in a few cases a cover takes on a life of its own and actually improves on the original. Such is the case with Hendrix's cover of Dylan's "All Along the Watchtower." It changed the way Dylan thought about the song too, and after Hendrix died, Dylan only played it Jimi's way. Other great covers: José

Feliciano's version of the Doors' "Light
My Fire." You'd think violins would
trash it, but they work. And Janis
Joplin belting out Kris Kristofferson's
"Me and Bobby McGee" defines the word
classic. He didn't know she'd covered
his song till he heard it the day after
she died. "Me and Bobby McGee" is only
the second posthumous #1 single in rock
history--but I'm not telling you what
the other one was.

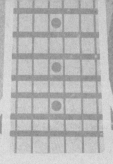

Breakup Songs
I Hope I Don't Have
to Listen To

★ "I Heard It Through the Grapevine"
—Marvin Gaye

★ "Crying"—Roy Orbison

★ "Yesterday"—The Beatles

★ "Heartbreak Hotel"—Elvis Presley

★ "49 Bye-Byes"—Crosby, Stills & Nash

★ "It's Too Late"—Carole King

★ "Babe, I'm Gonna Leave You"—Led Zeppelin

★ "Tracks of My Tears"—Smokey Robinson & the Miracles

★ "Ain't No Sunshine When She's Gone"—Bill Withers

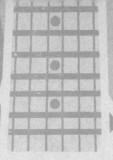

★ **"Love Hurts"**—The Everly Brothers

★ **"Don't Think Twice (It's All Right)"**
—Bob Dylan

★ **"Ain't Too Proud to Beg"**—The
Temptations

★ **"She's Not There"**—The Zombies

★ **"How Can You Mend a Broken Heart"**—The
Bee Gees

★ **"For No One"**—The Beatles

★ **"River"**—Joni Mitchell (For that matter, almost any Joni Mitchell song will do.)

For the next month on the way to school, I bring a Tupperware container full of leftover dinner to Brett. He always eats it quickly and is so grateful I feel bad I didn't bring him food from the beginning. He says he's been on the Strip looking for odd jobs and avoiding the police. I tell him my parents are usually out and there's a small bathroom with a shower in Dad's garage office. He tells me he doesn't want to impose, but we both know he's never going to find any pickup work looking the way he does now.

It's my first Valentine's Day with a girlfriend, which should be a joyous occasion, but instead of making cards and buying Caroline gifts, I'm still fixated on my Ouija buddies spelling out **S·H·E I·S U·N·H·A·P·P·Y**. (Truth be told, I'm also obsessed with John and Yoko cohosting *The Mike Douglas Show* every afternoon this week, which has me racing home from school like a crazy man.) I haven't gathered the courage to ask Caroline if she's unhappy; maybe Lynne is wrong, maybe Club 27 is wrong, or maybe . . . I'm losing my first girlfriend. We spend Valentine's evening watching *Laugh-In* and eating popcorn with her parents. I give her a pair of earrings my mother helped me pick out and she gives me Neil Young's *Harvest*, which came out just today. I have to force myself not to run home and put it on, but when I finally do I can't take it off. I lie in bed picking out the various artists singing background—ex-bandmates Crosby, Stills & Nash, as well as James Taylor and Linda Ronstadt. The new songs keep me from singing the Beach Boys' "Caroline, No," which has been running in a constant melancholic loop in my brain. *Where did your long hair go? Where is the girl I used to know. . . .* I bury my head in my pillow and try to fall asleep. Caroline and I just had a great night—why can't I ignore Club 27's predictions of doom?

The next morning before school, Caroline and I meet up at the newspaper office to collaborate on our column. I tell her I don't know what the hurry is, since my last few pieces have garnered no comments at all. NONE. (For anyone who's interested, the answer to the trivia tidbit in my last column about the first posthumous #1 hit was Otis Redding's "Dock of the Bay." NOT THAT ANYONE

CARES.) But Caroline's enthusiasm is contagious, and it doesn't take me long to start brainstorming. We decide not on a column per se, but a list of the best album covers of all time. I balk at first, thinking that saying anything is the best is like buying an artist's greatest hits album—as if a musician's essence can be diluted down to just his or her hits. I HATE THAT. But even I have to admit the idea is a good combination of my love of music trivia and Caroline's obsession with images, a solid subject for our first collaboration. And when the editor commits to giving us a full page in the paper with as many photos as we want, I get even more excited. It doesn't take long to come up with the list, which I edit throughout the day.

The principal announces that Mrs. Clarkson had a baby girl and named her Jasmine. I'm glad for Mrs. Clarkson but wish she were coming back sooner than next year because Mr. Woodrow is officially driving me crazy. It's infuriating the way he sits on Mrs. Clarkson's desk pontificating about the war as if there's nothing else going on in current events. I mean, how long can you talk about the Pentagon Papers? But with Brett still here, I have to admit the war is creeping into my daily life—and that's not a good thing.

Caroline, on the other hand, practically worships Woodrow, bringing in all kinds of photos and articles from the newspaper for the class to talk about. He holds up one now, a famous photo from a few years ago of a general in Vietnam executing a guy in the middle of the street at close range.

"This is General Nguyen Ngoc Loan killing a member of the Vietcong. Eddie Adams took this picture—it's one of the most brutal images from the war so far."

I don't know how Caroline got her hands on an eight-by-ten glossy of this horrific execution, but Mr. Woodrow passes it around the room for all of us to see. When it gets to me, I look closely and can actually see the bullet exiting the poor guy's head. I pass it back to Ashley feeling like I might get sick.

"Can we talk about something else?" I ask Mr. Woodrow. "Like that plane getting hijacked?" I know I'm not the only one in class fascinated with a guy named D. B. Cooper, who kidnapped a Boeing 727 in Washington state then parachuted off the plane with $200,000 in cash. The FBI kicked off one of the largest manhunts in national history—certainly this constitutes a current event too. But before I get a chance to rally any classmates to this new choice of topic, Mr. Woodrow cuts me off at the knees.

"Let me get this straight," he says. "You'd rather talk about a publicity stunt than a U.S. ally executing a prisoner in broad daylight?"

WELL, WHEN YOU PUT IT THAT WAY. I look over at Caroline, who seems embarrassed to know me. Am I imagining things or does she shoot Ryan a quick look too?

But Woodrow tastes blood and he doesn't let go. "You're a big music guy, right, Quinn? I heard you talking about Hendrix and Morrison—are these guys your heroes?"

I fold my hands across my chest and feel the rest of the class's eyes on me. I refuse to answer his question.

"Hendrix was in the army—a horrible soldier, they finally kicked him out. And Morrison?" He turns to face the rest of the class. "He walked into the induction office wasted and talked his way out of serving. Meanwhile, his father is an admiral in the navy—did you know that? As high up as you can get. Remember when we talked about the Gulf of Tonkin? Morrison's father was in charge of the naval fleet there while his son's fans were dying by the thousands. Nice family, huh?"

Some of the kids have tuned out Woodrow's rant; others look on in horror. Lindy rolls her eyes as if he's crazy and I'm just a deer caught in his crosshairs. But the two people I look to for support—Ryan and Caroline—have both turned away, not making eye contact with Woodrow or me. The fact that neither of them lifts a finger to help infuriates me more than Woodrow's diatribe.

But I don't take the tirade lying down. "I don't know if any of that's true. I'm going to ask both of them when I get home."

A few of my Ouija customers snicker, and Woodrow bends forward from the desk. "Excuse me?"

In my hurry to defend myself, I've let my Ouija connection slip. I immediately backpedal. "My mother's friend knew both of them. I'll ask her."

Caroline finally raises her hand. "Can you tell us about the Gulf of Tonkin incident again? I must've been out that day 'cuz I don't remember it."

My is-she-or-is-she-not-my-girlfriend has finally stepped in to change the subject. When I look over at Willy, he makes his fingers into a gun and points to his head. Ryan is regrettably still silent, drumming his fingers on his desk. When I do catch his eye, he shrugs as if the whole thing is no big deal. But it is a big deal, another nail in the coffin of our relationship.

Turns out this incident with the USS *Maddox* in the Gulf of Tonkin led Congress to pass a resolution giving the president legal justification to start open warfare against North Vietnam, really escalating the fighting. Woodrow goes on until the bell rings, which is literally music to my ears.

But Woodrow motions for me as I race to the door. Do I pretend I don't see him and blow him off? The last thing I want to do is irritate him more, so I slowly approach the desk.

"Sorry if I came down on you back then," he says. "You just really got my goat with that D. B. Cooper comment. These days it's the outlaws—the bank robbers, the rock stars—who get all the accolades, while the working folk, the guys actually fighting the war, are totally for-gotten. People are getting killed while you kids are safe at home watching *The Monkees*."

"How can anybody forget about the war?" I ask. "The nightly news is acres of body bags."

"That's my point—nobody knows who *those* kids are. They're anonymous, while these other guys are household names." Mr. Woodrow shakes his head as he stares out the window. "None of the young men in those body bags could even vote on this war until last June. Hopefully next election, the rest of you kids will come out in droves." It's almost as if Mr. Woodrow's forgotten I'm standing right here as he continues to look outside. "Rich men sending poor men to war—always has been, always will be."

"I guess I never thought about it that way before," I suddenly think about Brett, who no longer seems like one of my sister's friends looking for a handout but one link in a chain of people being asked to fight causes they can't articulate.

"We're not going to fix this problem today," Mr. Woodrow says. "See you tomorrow, Quinn."

And just like that, Mr. Woodrow goes from the person I dislike most in the world to one I can almost understand.

I feel like a moron asking Club 27 about the Gulf of Tonkin incident, but it turns out Mr. Woodrow was right. Morrison's father WAS an admiral and the commander of the naval forces there. The randomness of having the dad of one of rock's biggest stars actively involved in a war his son drank and sang his way through is mind-boggling. Not that Morrison should've been by his father's side—I'm not sure anyone should be anymore.

Mr. Woodrow was right about Hendrix too; he got kicked out of the military after a few months. The army's loss was certainly rock and roll's gain, but the whole thing just makes me sad. I wish Soosie were here so we could talk about it. I always make fun of the way she eats and breathes every facet of the war as if it's as integral to her daily life as flossing. Of course I hardly ever floss—maybe that's part of the problem.

FOR WHAT IT'S WORTH

3/72

Stephen Stills auditioned for the role of one of the Monkees but got turned down, so he recommended his friend Peter Tork for the role. Peter--who has one of the biggest party houses in the Canyon--got the role when he accidentally walked into a wall on the audition, demonstrating the kind of slapstick energy the producers were looking for. Mike Nesmith hosts the

Monday Night Hootenanny at the
Troubadour and has introduced many of
L.A.'s hottest bands. His mom is no
slouch either; working as a secretary,
she invented the correction fluid Liquid
Paper. Micky Dolenz had to learn to play
drums for the gig; Davy Jones was a
good drummer, but because he was so
short, no one could see him behind the
kit. Davy was nominated for a Tony
Award for his portrayal of the Artful
Dodger in <u>Oliver</u> on Broadway. The cast
performed on <u>The Ed Sullivan Show</u> the
same night as the Beatles' historic
first appearance. Watching the girls in
the audience screaming for John, Paul,

George, and
Ringo, Davy
decided right
then and there
what he wanted
to do with the
rest of his
life.

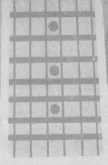

Anti-War Songs

★ "I Ain't Marchin' Anymore"—Phil Ochs

★ "War"—Edwin Starr

★ "Eve of Destruction"—Barry McGuire

★ "Give Peace a Chance"—John Lennon and the Plastic Ono Band

★ "Blowin' in the Wind"—Bob Dylan

★ "Fortunate Son"—Creedence Clearwater Revival

★ "What's Going On?"—Marvin Gaye

★ "I-Feel-Like-I'm-Fixin'-to-Die Rag"—Country Joe McDonald and the Fish

★ "Universal Soldier"—Donovan

★ "Peace Train"—Cat Stevens

★ **"Save the Country"**—The 5th Dimension

★ **"Masters of War"**—Bob Dylan

★ **"This Land Is Your Land"**—Woody Guthrie

★ **"I Don't Wanna to Be a Soldier"**—John Lennon

★ **"Machine Gun"**—Jimi Hendrix

★ **"Compared to What"**—Les McCann

It takes me twenty minutes to pick out the right T-shirt for my meeting with Zappa. A concert tee seems too obvious, especially one of his. Maybe it's the remnants of my conversation with Mr. Woodrow, but I choose the shirt with the flower that reads WAR IS NOT HEALTHY FOR CHILDREN OR OTHER LIVING THINGS. It was hardly worth the fuss because the last thing Frank focuses on is my wardrobe.

He examines each sheet of music carefully. When he finally looks up, he's smiling. "You do good work."

"Coming from you, that means a lot."

He puts the sheets in the old-fashioned briefcase he's carrying. "You want to do some more?"

"Absolutely!" I hadn't even let myself dream about doing more transcriptions for him and am even more surprised when he goes inside the Canyon Store for two sodas and sits down to chat as if he doesn't have anyplace more important to be. He talks about the new song he's working on, his kids, the European tour he just got back from. He talks about David Bowie covering his song "It Can't Happen Here." I tell him I just heard Deep Purple's "Smoke on the Water," where they mention Frank Zappa and the Mothers. It seems when Zappa and his band were playing a gig in Switzerland, some bozo in the audience set off a flare that burned the whole place down. Deep Purple—in town to record the next day—sat and watched the smoke roll across Lake Geneva from their hotel room. Frank lost all his equipment, but it looks like Deep Purple is scoring a monster hit out of the tragedy. What an opening riff!

Why can't every kid in my class come by as I'm sitting here talking rock and roll with one of the coolest guys in the city? And why does Zappa have that stray patch of hair underneath his bottom lip?

Zappa motions up Laurel Canyon Boulevard. "We used to live in the cabin at the corner of Lookout Mountain Avenue. It got so crazy, we had to move."

I know exactly where he means—cars used to park along the street for miles for his legendary parties. For someone who doesn't drink or do drugs, Zappa is certainly an odd choice for the center of the rock-and-roll party scene.

"People used to come and go all hours of the day and night. We didn't stay there long."

I decide not to tell him about my Ouija connection with Club 27, even though he probably knew all three of them. I'm not sure what Frank would make of my supernatural portal.

He leans back and takes a long sip of soda. "I still miss the bowling alley in the basement, the treehouse too. Did you know Houdini used to live across the street in the twenties? He supposedly had séances there to try and talk to his dead mother."

Now THIS is interesting.

"There were all these tunnels and underground rooms. A person could get lost."

A metaphorical lightbulb appears above my head. I take a deep breath before asking my next question. "Does anyone live there now?"

"Been empty for a while. Landlord's waiting for the right tenant, I guess." He reaches into his back pocket for several folded bills, then hands me another tape from his briefcase.

"Here's more if you want. My number's on there. Call me when you're done."

Not only do I have a JOB, I have a job in the MUSIC INDUSTRY WORKING FOR FRANK ZAPPA. (Not to mention a nice chunk of change for my album collection.) My worries about keeping Caroline, harboring Brett, and the escalating war suddenly evaporate. I ride over to Caroline's as soon as Frank drives away.

I step cautiously into her backyard, hoping not to relive finding Ryan there. She's sitting on a chair near the olive tree with a lapful of string.

"I'm making you a bracelet. See?" She holds up four inches of woven white string.

I examine the neat, even pattern. Besides my aunt Tamara making me a quilt when I was born, I don't think anyone has ever made me a present before. I kiss her and decide to listen to my heart instead of Lynne and Club 27. "Come on. I have someone to introduce you to."

"Is it Frank?" She jumps out of her chair.

I tell her maybe she can meet Zappa next time. She climbs onto the back of my banana seat and we head to my house to pick up some food. When we finally get to the woods, it takes fifteen minutes to locate Brett. He waves shyly to Caroline, but I can see all he's focused on is the aluminum foil packet in my hands. He devours the roasted chicken and potatoes in seconds.

"Who is he?" Caroline whispers.

I give her the abridged version while Brett licks his fingers clean.

"You're a draft dodger?" she asks.

I shoot her a look to be cool while Brett tells her he is.

"My brother didn't want to go to war either, but he's

in Vietnam now, not hiding out in Laurel Canyon eating chicken."

For someone who carries a Kent State photo on her notebook, I'm surprised by Caroline's reaction and pull her aside. "What are you doing? I'm helping him. I thought you'd be proud—he's a war resister."

"My brother's hiking through rice paddies with fifty pounds of stuff on his back while people shoot at him with machine guns. He wanted to resist too, but he didn't."

I hate to remind her what actually happened but have to. "Uhm, your brother went 'cuz your father made him."

Brett waves his hands in the air as if he's sorry the two of us are fighting. "My father wanted me to go too. I just couldn't. And my draft board rejected conscientious objector in almost every case, so I got scared." He looks at Caroline with an expression of such kindness it makes me realize why Soosie took the time to get to know this quiet guy behind a deli counter slicing cheese. "I don't want to kill anyone—it's that simple."

"It's *not* that simple," Caroline says. "You think my brother wants to kill people? He won't use a flyswatter."

I've never seen Caroline so mad, and I suddenly wonder if I've put Brett in a dangerous position. Will she call the police and turn him in? I decide to give Caroline a ride home before the tension gets any thicker. I tell Brett I'll see him tomorrow.

As I put my feet down to steady my bike at the red

light, I realize this is the intersection Frank talked about earlier. I've never been on the property, although I know Soosie went to several parties here. As I pedal past the stockade fence surrounding the large unoccupied yard and cabin, I know just where to relocate Brett.

"I'm sorry I overreacted." Caroline climbs off the bike in front of her house. "Don't worry. I won't turn him in." I tell her I didn't think she would, even though that's exactly what I WAS thinking. I give her a quick kiss goodbye, then pedal home.

When I throw my shirt into the laundry later, I run my hand across the silkscreened words. WAR IS NOT HEALTHY FOR CHILDREN OR OTHER LIVING THINGS. My mother got me the shirt because it was on sale; I liked the childlike handwriting and the hippie vibe, never really thinking about its message. But things are different now. I've been telling myself I'm just bringing leftovers to my sister's friend, but truth be told, I'm aiding a war resister, even helping him find a place to crash. The war has crept into my life more than I ever thought it would; after this, I want to go back to minding my own business, listening to my records, and transcribing songs. When I toss my shirt into the hamper, it misses and falls to the floor.

My Ouija friends only make matters worse. **S-H-E I-S H-I-D-I-N-G S-O-M-E-T-H-I-N-G**, they say.

"She's making me a bracelet! Our column comes out tomorrow!" I yell at the board. "What can she possibly be hiding?"

Club 27 is bumming me out. I wonder if I'd have better luck with Houdini.

FOR WHAT IT'S WORTH

3/72

David Jones came up with his stage name
David Bowie to get a fresh start after
several failed attempts with local
bands--and being confused with Davy
Jones of Monkees fame. He took his new
last name from Jim Bowie, an American
pioneer who died at the Alamo. Besides
helping to give a British pop star his
pseudonym, Jim Bowie also lent his name
to the Bowie knife because of his skill

with the blade. Many people think David
Bowie was born with two different-
colored eyes--one blue and one hazel--
but the reason they're different is
because he got punched in the eye
by one of his best friends when he was
young. He missed eight months of school
and was almost blinded; one eye was
left permanently dilated. Surprisingly,
the guy who punched Bowie remained his
friend and ended up doing the artwork
for several of his albums.

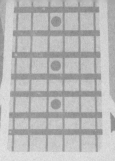

My Favorite Album Covers of All Time—in no particular order

★ **Who's Next**—The Who

★ **English Rose**—Fleetwood Mac

★ **We're Only in It for the Money**—Frank Zappa and the Mothers of Invention

★ **Atom Heart Mother**—Pink Floyd

★ **Led Zeppelin III**—Led Zeppelin

★ **Strange Days**—The Doors

★ **Ogdens' Nut Gone Flake**—The Small Faces

★ **Blind Faith**—Blind Faith

★ **Sticky Fingers**—The Rolling Stones

★ **Trout Mask Replica**—Captain Beefheart

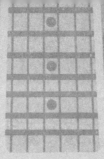

★ **Whipped Cream and Other Delights**—Herb Albert's Tijuana Brass

★ **The Beatles** (aka **The White Album**)—The Beatles

★ **Emerson, Lake & Palmer**—Emerson, Lake & Palmer

★ **Cheap Thrills**—Janis Joplin with Big Brother & the Holding Company

★ **The Freewheelin' Bob Dylan**—Bob Dylan

★ **In the Court of the Crimson King**—King Crimson

★ **Sketches of Spain**—Miles Davis

★ **Black Sabbath**—Black Sabbath

★ **Revolver**—The Beatles

★ **Tarkus**—Emerson, Lake & Palmer

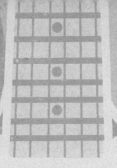

★ **Mott the Hoople**—Mott the Hoople

★ **Magical Mystery Tour**—The Beatles

★ **Hot Rats**—Frank Zappa

★ **A Saucerful of Secrets**—Pink Floyd

★ **Days of Future Passed**—The Moody Blues

★ **American Beauty**—The Grateful Dead

★ **Hot Buttered Soul**—Isaac Hayes

★ **Disraeli Gears**—Cream

★ **Abbey Road**—The Beatles

★ **Abraxas**—Santana

★ **Weasels Ripped My Flesh**—Frank Zappa and the Mothers of Invention

★ **Fragile**—Yes

★ **Tommy**—The Who

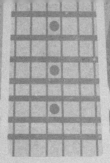

★ **The Low Spark of High Heeled Boys**—Traffic

★ **Sergeant Pepper**—The Beatles

★ **The Who Sell Out**—The Who

★ **Aoxomoxa**—The Grateful Dead

★ **Sailin' Shoes**—Little Feat

★ **Let It Bleed**—The Rolling Stones

★ **If You Can Believe Your Eyes and Ears**—The Mamas and the Papas

★ **Clouds**—Joni Mitchell

★ **Odyssey and Oracle**—The Zombies

★ **Axis: Bold as Love**—The Jimi Hendrix Experience

★ **Forever Changes**—Love

The smog is so thick today, Mom and I can't see the mountains from the 405.

"Laurie went for a jog yesterday and had to stop after half a mile—the air quality was so bad, she couldn't even breathe," Mom says.

"Why would somebody jog anyway? Was she being chased?"

My mother laughs in agreement. "It's the newest thing. But I do worry about all this air pollution, don't you?"

I don't tell her how I've been obsessed by the Keep America Beautiful commercial with the Native American crying at all the water pollution. The other day, Mr. Woodrow—who can't keep current events out of any lesson plan—told us about a river in Ohio that spontaneosly

BURST INTO FLAMES a few years ago because of all the debris and oil on its surface. He said the incident helped create the new environmental movement, but all I kept wondering was HOW MUCH TRASH DOES THERE HAVE TO BE FOR A RIVER TO CATCH ON FIRE? No wonder that Native American guy is crying.

"Are things all right with school and Caroline?" Mom asks. "Did people like the column?"

I tell her the paper got the biggest response they've ever had and Patty asked us to do another list for the big issue at the end of the year. My mother puts her psycho-analysis experience to good use. "Let's see—you're happy about the positive feedback but wish people had made such a fuss about your regular column. Hmmm?"

I hate it when she's right about these things.

She senses I don't want to talk about it further and asks me how the band is doing instead. I tell her we find out today if we get to play at the school dance.

"What are you calling yourself now?"

"Last week it was Broken Flip-Flop, but now we're Three-Legged Dog."

She presses the lighter into the console to heat it up again.

"I thought one of the reasons you started psycho-analysis was to quit smoking?"

As the traffic slows, she holds the burning coil to the

Virginia Slim dangling from her lips. "Smoking is so far down the list of things I'm processing right now."

I turn away from the smoke and lean my head against the window. The last thing I want to listen to after getting two cavities filled is whatever is going on inside my mother's head. When I hear the opening chords to Cat Stevens's "Father and Son" on the radio, I crank up the volume. My mother likes this song too and sings along, nudging me to join in. Like analyzing lyrics in English class, singing in the car with your mother is pretty much something to be avoided at all costs.

As we sit at the red light at Laurel Canyon and Lookout Mountain, I nonchalantly gaze out my window. I helped Brett settle into the cabin a few days ago and I'm hoping he's doing okay. Translation—I pray my work with him is done.

I'm half an hour late when Mom drops me at Willy's for practice. I told Willy and Ryan that I couldn't get out of my dentist appointment and would come as soon as I could, so I'm surprised to find Caroline already there.

"I thought I was going to see you later."

She's sitting cross-legged on the stone wall outside Willy's garage. "I just figured I'd meet you here. Is that okay?"

I nod, not wanting to drool on myself from the Novocain.

"We're trying to learn 'Doctor My Eyes,'" Ryan says.

Luckily it's a Jackson Browne song I've played before so I won't look like too much of a hack in front of Caroline. Willy counts us off, but we don't make it past the first verse before Ryan stops singing.

"I hope we *don't* get the stupid gig at school," he says. "'Cuz we couldn't play for an hour if our lives depended on it."

"Starting a band was YOUR idea," I say. "It was all you talked about for months, but as soon as the hard part comes, you want to bail."

"I don't want to quit but we suck." Ryan unplugs his guitar from the amp.

"You can't quit now," Willy adds. "We just got started."

"Come on, let's try it one more time." I can't figure out what's eating Ryan—we don't sound THAT bad.

In all the times I fantasized about being in a band, I never thought about how long the learning curve would be. On a day when we're not clicking, practice is about as much fun as HOMEWORK. I'd imagined Ryan and I would weave guitars back and forth, dueling leads, but in reality, our timing is off and sometimes it feels as if we're playing different songs. Do we need more practice or are we never going to gel?

Thankfully, Ryan plugs his guitar back in and we

make it through the song three times before taking a break. Caroline approaches me with her hands behind her back, then places the bracelet in my hands.

"Do you like it?" Her nose is scrunched up as if I might not.

I examine the detail of the white woven string—she really did a great job. It looks like the "anti-shark" bracelets they sell at the shops in Malibu. I tell her I love it.

"I'm so glad!" She reaches into her bag, takes out another three bracelets, and hands them to Willy, Ryan, and Marvin.

"You made us ALL bracelets?"

"They're bard bracelets," she says. "You guys can wear them for your gigs."

Willy has a well-worn similar bracelet on his left wrist and is excited to now have one for his right. Ryan and Marvin slip theirs on too, but I feel unsettled and selfish inside. Shouldn't I be happy that my girlfriend thinks enough about me to go the extra mile and make presents for my bandmates too? She put a lot of time in—I should appreciate that, right? Instead of focusing on the fact that all her effort wasn't being lavished on me? I'm not sure how it's possible for such an altruistic moment to transform into one of self-flagellation, but in the wonderful world of QUINN'S FEEBLE MIND, that's what happens. I tell myself to stop thinking like a cretin and keep focused on the song.

Maybe it's to pay her back for making the band bracelets, but Willy invites Caroline to sing backup. Before I get a chance to tell her she doesn't have to, Caroline joins Ryan and me at our only mic. My voice is passable, Ryan's a bit better, but when Caroline comes in on the chorus, the look on Willy's face is one of shock. I know what he's thinking because I've thought it too—how can such a smart, cute girl sing so badly? I feel my cheeks redden and want to stop the song before anyone makes fun of her. But Caroline is LOVING this, singing her guts out. "I . . . am everyday people." Is it fair to curtail someone's enthusiasm just because she's bad? (And when I say bad, I mean, god-awful, horrific, terrible.) Willy, Marvin, and Ryan fight back laughter and I have to admire Caroline for choosing joy over what other people think. By the end of the song, I admire her even more than I usually do.

"Well, *that* was interesting," Willy says when we're done.

"How about one more?" Caroline asks.

I make up an excuse about having to stop by my mother's store and pack up my guitar. Caroline needs no excuse to flip through Mom's racks of clothes and comes along.

"I know I can't sing," she says as we walk. "But I *love* to. Thanks for letting me join in even though I stink."

As her boyfriend, what do I do here? Am I supposed

to say she DOESN'T stink when all the evidence points to the contrary? I tell her I love it when she comes to rehearsal, which is 100 percent true.

When we get to the store, Tanya says Mom's having lunch with my father and will be back in an hour. But this news doesn't stop Caroline, who grabs four hangers full of blouses to try on. (I really can't complain; I've dragged her to the record store almost every Tuesday—new release day—since we've been going out.)

Caroline buys a gauzy pink shirt with the proceeds from our Club 27 project. Thanks to her efforts, our business has increased to almost a dozen kids a week, which has been a boon for Caroline's wardrobe, as well as my record collection. (What to get this week—Ry Cooder's *Into the Purple Valley*? Stevie Wonder's *Music of My Mind*?) When Tanya finds out Caroline made my bracelet, she gushes over her macramé skills and says she'll talk to my mother about carrying them in the store—yet another moneymaking opportunity, which causes Caroline to try on one more blouse.

As we walk back up Sunset, Caroline ducks inside an alley and makes me barricade the sun as she loads film into her camera. She snaps photos of the telephone wires, the shampoo bottles lined up in the drugstore window, and graffiti scrawled on the side of a motel. We have a great afternoon, mostly because I ignore Club 27's stupid predictions that she's going to leave.

I remember a book my mother keeps on the coffee table at home: *Be Here Now.* It's got a deep blue cover and the pages look like the brown paper they make lunch bags out of. I've flipped through it—the message is basically about living in the present without a lot of baggage in your head. Lately I feel like I've got a full set of luggage up there; I had no idea having a girlfriend took up such a giant chunk of your brain. (Although to be fair, the band and the war Mr. Woodrow won't stop talking about contribute to that too.) I snap myself out of this downward spiral—if I don't get out of my head and start living in the real world soon, I AM going to lose my girlfriend.

"You okay?" Caroline asks.

I tell her I'm fine but have to bring Brett some dinner.

"He can't stay here forever," she says. "Did he decide if he's going to Canada?"

"He was planning to hitchhike, but I think he's worried about people who pick him up getting into trouble since he's wanted by the authorities. He's trying to save up enough for a bus."

"Yeah, but once he gets there, how's he going to cross the border? Won't his name come up at customs?"

"Well, aren't you all informed?" I snatch the camera and snap a quick picture of her trying to grab it out of my hand.

When we get to the top of her street, I thank her again for the bracelet, then correct myself. "I mean bracelets—you didn't have to make them for all of us." And when I say "all of us," I mostly mean Ryan, who's had girls making him stuff since grade school.

When I get back home, I'm surprised to see Dad.

"I thought you were having lunch with Mom."

"We went to the Farmers' Market. I always forget to go—I like it there." He motions toward a bag on the counter. "Brought you back some leftovers."

Black beans and rice in the middle of the afternoon— a real treat. I finish it off while Dad gets out the lawn mower.

"You want to play Frisbee?" he asks.

I look over at my father—it's hard to believe Soosie ever thought he'd turn Brett in to the authorities. His wire glasses are crooked, he's got a red bandanna with grease spots hanging out of his pocket, and his work-boots look like he dug them out of a Dumpster. He's about the least threatening guy I know. Should I defy my older sister and tell him about Brett? Take him over to Zappa's old place now and introduce them?

When the phone rings, my father waves me inside as if he already knows getting to the phone is ten times more important to me than playing Frisbee.

"We got the gig!" Willy says.

YES! This is the first official gig for Drawn & Quartered—we came up with yet another name this afternoon—and we've got a lot of work to do before the dance. I tell Willy I'll see him after dinner to work on some songs before tomorrow's practice.

"Dad!" I shout into the yard. "We got our first gig!"

My father shuts off the lawn mower and tells me he didn't hear a word I said. It doesn't bother me to repeat the news—a few dozen more times.

The set list is obviously of paramount importance. Do we open with "Lola" or "Brown Sugar"? "Proud Mary" or "If You Really Love Me?"

It's a dance, so you have to have a FEW slow songs, but which ones? "Mercy, Mercy Me" or "I Believe in You"?

What do we do during our break—besides wait for people to come up and tell us how great we are?

POMP AND CIRCUMSTANCE RULE!

(We changed our name again.)

FOR WHAT IT'S WORTH

9/72

Neil Young wrote three of his biggest
songs for Everybody Knows This Is
Nowhere--"Cinnamon Girl," "Down by the
River," and "Cowgirl in the Sand"--all
on the same day while sick in bed with
a 103-degree fever. He's never really
been healthy: he has diabetes and
epilepsy and even had polio as a kid.

A Canadian citizen, Young drove to
L.A. in his hearse. He was on Sunset

Boulevard when Stephen Stills saw him
drive by with his friend Bruce Palmer.
Stills and Richie Furay had been
looking all over town for musicians to
start a band with. When Stills saw the
hearse with Ontario plates, he knew it
was Neil, whom he'd met while
performing in Canada. He and Furay did
a U-turn on Sunset, pulled over Neil,
and--presto--Buffalo Springfield was
born. They took their name from a
steamroller they saw parked on their
producer's street.

Brett met a woman from Silver Lake who's letting him crash at her place for a while, freeing up Zappa's old cabin. I debate whether to tell the band about it as a possible place to practice, but visions of real estate agents and police officers squash the idea pretty quickly. I swear I have NO ULTERIOR MOTIVES when I take Caroline there after school.

"Why do you keep looking over your shoulder?" Caroline asks.

"Because we're not supposed to be here, that's why." I give her a boost to climb over the fence, then scale it myself. (Is she paying attention to how coordinated and strong I am?)

I know Soosie's been here before, but I'm floored by what I see, an oasis right off one of the busiest streets in the Canyon. Large wooden tree houses, a pond, giant trees—the place is huge, probably several acres. I tamp down the thought that says YOU'RE TRESPASSING, grab Caroline's hand, and wander around like we're guest stars on *Danger Island*.

We descend the old wooden stairs to an area that looks like a dungeon. A dungeon!

"There's a bowling alley down here," Caroline says. "And tunnels!"

I tell her the tunnels supposedly lead to Houdini's old house that burned down on the other side of the street. I tell her about the séances he used to have to contact the spirits. "Houdini spent years offering a reward to anyone who could make contact with the other side. He was always disappointed, though. Never got to talk to his mother."

Caroline's face suddenly lights up the entire basement, which is good because it's pretty scary down here.

"You talk to the dead all the time," she says.

"It's a Ouija board—it's not like I take it seriously."

She catches me in my lie. "Of course you take it seriously! If not, then why do you consult it all the time? And if you don't believe it's really Club 27, you should give our friends their money back." She gives my jacket a little tug.

"Okay, I'm superstitious, I believe in all that crazy stuff, but that doesn't mean I want to host a séance."

She continues to play with the hem of my jacket, and I suddenly get a jolt of excitement that our visit here might turn romantic.

But Caroline has something else in mind. "We should invite our clients—"

"They're not clients, they're our classmates."

She's on a roll and my words are barely a speed bump. "We should invite them all here for a séance—with Jimi, Janis, and Jim."

I tell her absolutely not, for a million reasons—namely that this place belongs to someone else. (I don't tell her one of my primary reasons is that it's creepy, dark, and strange.)

My comments fall on deaf ears. Like a director delegating to a gaggle of assistants, Caroline counts off all the things we'll have to do to prepare for such an event.

As darkness descends, I wonder about the coyote quotient in these gullies and hills and tell Caroline we have to go. Spirits, séances, the wind howling through broken branches? Not to sound like a wuss, but get me OUT of here.

Caroline—smarter than me even on her stupidest day—has another idea. "You want to help your sister's friend, right? We could charge for the séance, use the whole Houdini angle, and give all the proceeds to him. Then he can finally leave and you won't have to worry about him anymore."

I make sure the gate latches behind us. "You want to help me raise money for Brett?"

"Absolutely."

Is she serious? A while ago, I worried whether Caroline would turn him in. I tell her I'll have to think about it.

"You mean you have to run it by Club 27. Admit it—that's what you're thinking, right?"

The girl knows me too well. "I'll let you know what they say."

The second I get home, that's exactly what I do. As I slide the board out from underneath my bed, my mother enters my room and catches me red-handed.

"I was just cleaning up," I stammer.

She waves me off as if the Ouija is the last thing on her mind. "I just want to check in. Is everything okay?"

I slide the board back under my bed. "Everything's fine."

She sits at the foot of my bed. "Excited to play at the dance?"

"You're not going to come, are you? It'll make me nervous."

"Well, we don't want that." She gives me a tired smile. "How are things with Caroline?"

"Good."

"Ellen is having a party on Sunday afternoon if you want to come—you can bring Caroline too."

I nod as if this is the kind of exciting couples invitation I get all the time.

"I'm going to call Soosie—do you want to talk to her when I'm done?"

"Sure." I want to ask Soosie what she thinks about a fund-raiser for Brett and get some inside info on the Lookout Mountain place. But as soon as my mother leaves the room, I have a more pressing matter to attend to.

I place my fingers lightly on the planchette. I realize asking advice from three rock stars who died from abusing various illegal substances probably isn't the best plan, but I do it anyway. But before I even get to ask a question, the planchette begins to move. I say the letters out loud as the Ouija chooses them.

S·H·E C·A·N·T S·T·A·Y.

You're wrong, I think. She can stay—she WILL. And I decide to tell Caroline to go ahead and set up her stupid séance. If that'll make her happy, then that's what we'll do. I slap on my headphones and crank up some Kinks to seal the deal.

I know what you're thinking—that whole "if you love something, set it free" philosophy, right? I never liked that saying, never made a lick of sense to me. I'm going down fighting on this one.

FOR WHAT IT'S WORTH

The Kinks' third single "You Really
Got Me" was written by Ray Davies
and was a huge international hit, which
sent them to the studio to quickly
record their first album. The song got
its distorted dirty guitar sound from
Ray's brother Dave slashing the speaker
cone on his amp with a razor and
poking holes in it with a pin. The fuzz
from the vibrating fabric of the

speaker gave the song its indelible trashy riff; those killer power chords went on to influence lots of other bands, such as the Rolling Stones and The Who. And how old were they when they were creating that new sound? Ray was 20; Dave was 17.

My dad's working late, which makes it easier to sneak out of the house without a lot of explanations. Mom's got the living room full of boxes of clothes to inventory and barely looks up when I tell her I'll be at Caroline's. She doesn't notice that I'm carrying a bag filled with candles I've snatched from every room in the house.

When I get to the log cabin, Caroline's already there. She helps me distribute the candles throughout several of the underground rooms.

"This is going to be great," she says. "Tom, Lynne, Ashley, Willy, Ryan—"

"Ryan's not coming," I interrupt. "He hates anything supernatural."

"Well, he told me he *is* coming. Marvin too."

I feel even more stupid than I did before—I mean, I am a bit obsessed with the supernatural, but it's not usually something I discuss with my friends. Music, sure, that's a normal thing to talk about with other guys. But communicating with the dead? Not your basic conversation topic in the school lunch line.

"Did you bring the Ouija board?" Caroline asks.

I tell her I didn't, then watch her freak out.

"Calm down. Of course I did." I remove the board and planchette from my bag.

"Do you think we should try to get in touch with Houdini too?"

I shrug as if I don't care, but to be honest, I've given this whole séance thing a LOT of thought. Not just because I want the supernatural piece to go smoothly but because this is the closest thing to having a party at my house. Should there be music or will it interfere with the séance? Will kids be bored and want to leave early? I realize I'm making too big a deal over something that will probably only last an hour and tell myself to just have a good time.

"We should pick up some of this trash," Caroline says. "The wind's blown all these papers and leaves in."

I tell her no one's going to be looking at the décor and go to the gate when I hear Ryan, Willy, and Marvin.

"This is so cool," Ryan says. "Why don't we practice here?"

"How about tomorrow?" Marvin suggests.

I tell him there's no electricity.

"Acoustic," Willy answers. "We need to practice as much as we can before next Saturday."

Caroline hands Ryan a candle and leads the three of them down to the main room. A few minutes later, I'm shocked by the number of kids milling around the grotto. I ask Caroline how many she invited.

She shrugs. "Everyone from our class—at five dollars each, too."

"WHAT?"

"I'm going to start collecting. Is that okay?' she asks.

I suddenly feel like a deep-sea diver with the bends. TOO . . . MUCH . . . PRESSURE. I tell her to collect on the way out in case I screw up.

"Are you sure?" Caroline asks. "This is for Brett, remember?"

She's right, but I've been much more worried about Caroline breaking up with me than helping Brett, whom I haven't seen in a while. I pause on one of the footbridges to take some deep breaths. Have I taken this Club 27 thing too far? What started out as a lark now is a moneymaking proposition—suppose the Ouija doesn't work here, suppose some of the other kids think it's a hoax? If I knew how it worked, it would be one thing, but I don't have a clue. Suppose people don't like what they hear? Hey, I don't like what I hear half the time. If

Club 27 is wrong about Caroline, they can be wrong about anything, right?

"You ready, Houdini?" Ryan asks. "I hope you don't think I'm going to pay."

"This was Caroline's idea," I explain. "I've never done a séance before."

Ryan fake-punches me in the stomach, but all I can think of is that's how Houdini died. "You have to be open, right?"

He ushers me downstairs, where I take a quick head-count and come up with thirty-two. YIKES.

I pull a U-turn and face Ryan. "How about if we forget the séance and just play some of the songs we're doing for the dance?"

"What, a capella? We don't have any instruments." He gives me a little shove. "Go pull the wool over their eyes, Quinn."

Needless to say, I don't appreciate the put-down. When I look over at Caroline, she wears a "what are you waiting for?" expression.

Before sitting down next to her, I scan the room. The candles give off the only light in the basement and with all the shadows from the trees outside, the effect is dark and eerie. Most of the candles are my mom's clove votives from home, so the room smells like someone just baked fresh gingerbread—an aroma diametrically opposed to the scary visuals.

"I want to thank everyone for coming," I begin. "Tonight we're going to start off with a nod to Harry Houdini." I can see by his expression that Tom is disappointed we're not going straight to Hendrix.

Just as I take my seat, a breeze shoots in from the window and blows out several of the candles. A collective *ooooh* fills the room as Caroline and I relight them. I sit back down and realize the entire room is now holding hands. I grab Caroline's on one side and Ryan's on the other. (Were they holding hands before I sat down?)

When the shutter of the window bangs against the house, several of the girls scream—in a good, haunted-house way, not a help-I'm-getting-mugged kind of way. As much as I was reluctant to do this, tonight might turn out to be one of the main social events of the season.

I've always been superstitious and fascinated by the Ouija board, but I've never been to a séance, never mind orchestrating one. Thankfully, Kathye and Caroline pick up the lead and run.

"We invoke the spirits of Club 27." Caroline's voice is loud enough to be heard by the crowd, but still pretty low, almost sinister. I have to admit I'm a little taken aback.

"Jimi Hendrix, Janis Joplin, Jim Morrison," Kathye continues, "give us a sign you can hear us."

I dramatically place my hand on the planchette; Caroline joins me. For the first time in my Ouija career, nothing happens. The planchette sits there as if nailed to the board.

"Give us a sign," I say. I realize I can speed this process along by moving the planchette myself, but cheating now—in front of this many kids—doesn't seem like a smart move.

Even I'm surprised when the sign comes not from the immobile Ouija board but from the candles. Another gust breezes in, this time blowing out all the lights but one. It's either a coincidence or we really have stumbled on something. Goose bumps shoot up my arm as I realize I'm as much a spectator in this event as the other kids are. Girls are screaming, guys are laughing, but everyone can feel the suspense. Caroline reaches across the board to give my arm a squeeze, which sends another jolt through my already electric body.

We pick up the candles and light them again. I wait for everyone to settle down and return to the makeshift circle before speaking. "Jimi, Janis, and Jim, we know you're with us. This place is safe—please come back."

Even though there are more than thirty of us, you can literally hear a pin drop as we hold our collective breath. The rough-hewn logs, the dirt floor, the coyotes baying in the woods outside all add to the ambience and tension. None of the Hollywood production designers who live here in the Canyon could've come up with a better set.

I think I smell smoke but am thrown off by Lindy's moaning. Her low voice suddenly shifts to an ear-piercing scream as she backs out of the circle toward the wall.

"Morrison is here!" she shouts.

Several others start screaming now too—and not just girls. Willy knocks over a candle on his way to the exit; so does Maria. I force myself to turn around to see what's causing such fear. Through the panic, I see a hazy image of a guy with long, dark, wavy hair. He's got a round face, wide sideburns, and several days of stubble.

"It's Morrison," Ryan says. "He didn't die in Paris!"

"Or it's his ghost," Tom adds. "Where's Jimi—is he here too?"

The burning smell is now strong and the basement is full of smoke. I wave my arms to clear the air. Could this really be the work of Jim Morrison's ghost?

I peer through the increasing haze and realize it's not the Lizard King.

It's Brett.

"I came back to get some things," Brett says. "I didn't know you were having a party."

Ryan still stares as if I'm standing in the middle of Zappa's old basement having a conversation with Jim Morrison, back from the dead. With lots of trepidation, Ryan extends his hand to Brett. "I'm a big fan, always have been."

Brett turns to me in confusion. "What's going on?"

What brings me back to reality isn't Brett's question but Caroline tugging at my arm. "Those papers caught on fire—it's spreading. Come on! We have to get someone to call the fire department!"

I have taken off my jacket and started beating back the flames when I hear sirens racing across the Canyon.

"All that screaming and smoke—someone called the police," Caroline says. "We've got to get out of here."

I realize that as much trouble as we're all going to be in, the one with the most to lose is Brett. "Run!" I yell through the confusion.

He looks around for his things, but I push him out of the room. "Go!"

He reluctantly runs upstairs with Caroline. When I realize Ryan is still in the basement, I stumble through the haze to find him.

"Ryan!" I yell through the smoke. "Come on!"

I grab him by the shirt and pull him upstairs. "I *knew* he wasn't dead," Ryan says. "Knew he couldn't stay away."

I want to tell Ryan what he witnessed was not some rock-and-roll apparition but my sister's friend from Boston. But the explanation will have to wait because as soon as I climb over the fence onto Lookout Mountain Avenue, I am face-to-face with four of L.A.P.D.'s finest.

Who do you think was maddest—my parents, who grounded me for a month?

The principal of the junior high, who banned us from playing the dance?

The police, who found Brett's bag with his ID inside and are now searching all over town to bring him in on his warrant?

The owner of the property, who was there with insurance inspectors and locksmiths all week?

Ryan, when he found out his I-HAD-AN-ENCOUNTER-WITH-A-DEAD-ROCK-STAR story was utter hogwash?

Caroline at Brett for ruining our séance? Or at me for not helping her clean up the newspapers beforehand? Or for not letting her collect everyone's fee up front?

Or me—mad at myself for the police finding out

about Brett? Losing privileges for a month, not to mention MY PARENTS CONFISCATING MY ALBUMS AND OUIJA BOARD?

Flip a coin, join the club. EVERYBODY's mad at yours truly.

FOR WHAT IT'S WORTH

5/72

Sri Yukteswar Giri, Aleister Crowley,
Mae West, Lenny Bruce, Karlheinz
Stockhausen, W. C. Fields, Carl Jung,
Edgar Allan Poe, Fred Astaire, Richard
Merkin, the Vargas Girl, Huntz Hall,
Simon Rodia, Bob Dylan, Aubrey
Beardsley, Sir Robert Peel, Aldous
Huxley, Dylan Thomas, Terry Southern,
Dion, Tony Curtis, Wallace Berman, Tommy
Handley, Marilyn Monroe, William S.

Burroughs, Sri Mahavatar Babaji, Stan
Laurel, Richard Lindner, Oliver Hardy,
Karl Marx, H. G. Wells, Sri Paramahansa
Yogananda, Sigmund Freud, Stuart
Sutcliffe, Max Miller, "Petty Girl,"
Marlon Brando, Tom Mix, Oscar Wilde,
Tyrone Power, Larry Bell, Dr. David
Livingstone, Johnny Weissmuller, Stephen
Crane, Issy Bonn, George Bernard Shaw,
H. C. Westermann, Albert Stubbins,
Sri Lahiri Mahasaya, Lewis Carroll,
T. E. Lawrence, Sonny Liston, George
Harrison, John Lennon, Shirley Temple,
Ringo Starr, Paul McCartney, Albert
Einstein, Bobby Breen, Marlene Dietrich,
an American legionnaire, Diana Dors,
and Shirley Temple again.

Since I'm grounded with no music and
no guitar, I'm sitting at the library
with a record, an encyclopedia, and
microfiche identifying all the people on
the cover of Sgt. Peppers--the closest I
can get to appreciating an album without
listening to it. What a great way to
spend a Saturday afternoon. Yippee!

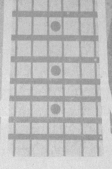

Songs to Sing at the Top of Your Lungs When You're Grounded

★ "We're Not Gonna Take It"—The Who

★ "We Gotta Get Out of This Place"—The Animals

★ "Ballad of Dwight Fry"—Alice Cooper

★ "White Room"—Cream

★ "Paint It Black"—The Rolling Stones

★ "My Generation"—The Who

★ "Like a Rolling Stone"—Bob Dylan

★ "In My Room"—The Beach Boys

★ "(I Can't Get No) Satisfaction"—The Rolling Stones (The Stones versus The Who: which band writes the best songs for disaffected youth? I vote The Who, but you decide.)

My mother goes into overdrive at her analyst's, blaming herself for not being around enough in the past few months. I tell her that even if she'd been here every second, it wouldn't have changed the situation with Brett. She and my father spend many mornings on the phone with Soosie, who's in almost as much trouble as I am. Her finals ended this week and she's driving home for the summer—a fine cross-country trip THAT's going to be.

"Don't tell Mom and Dad," she says when she gets me alone on the phone, "but I'm coming home to sell the van. We have to find Brett and help him get out of the States before they arrest him. If I know him, he's ready to turn himself in—the last thing he ever wants to do is cause anybody any trouble."

"Well, he caused me a TON of trouble."

"You shouldn't have thrown a party at the cabin," Soosie says. "Or started a fire. That's on you, not Brett."

I tell her for the millionth time I wouldn't have been there in the first place if I hadn't been looking for a place to hide her friend. "You owe me big time."

"I'll be home next week," she says. "Just worry about finding him."

The days go by like a prison sentence. I'm depressed about losing my albums but am surprised by how much I miss the band. It's almost like Willy, Ryan, and Marvin use getting busted as an excuse to throw in the towel. Sure, practicing is a lot of work and we aren't good yet, but won't it be worth the effort in the end? I mean, what else do we have to do with our time? I spend hours on the phone with all three of them trying to change their minds, but with summer on the horizon, everyone but me votes to call it quits for a while. I lick my wounds by playing guitar alone for hours every afternoon.

After dinner, I go out to the porch to find my parents waiting for me. Great, yet another interrogation about Brett.

"I don't understand why you didn't come to us," my father says. "Did you really think I was going to put on my old navy whites and march him over to the induction center?" He actually seems hurt. "I'm against this war as much as you are."

"You've been more informed lately, which is good," Mom adds. "I don't know if it's because of Mr. Woodrow or Brett, but it seems like you're at least *thinking* about the war now. So there's *that* to be grateful for." My mother mindlessly braids her hair with deft fingers as she talks. "That poor boy should've stayed in Soosie's room, not hidden in the woods like an animal—I still feel bad about that."

"Hold on," my father says. "He couldn't have stayed here—we'd have been aiding and abetting a felon. He might be a friend of Soosie's, but he's not worth going to prison for."

"We wouldn't have stood by while one of our daughter's friends needed help."

"He's *his* parents' problem, not ours." My father grasps the arms of the chair to steady his anger.

"THIS is why I didn't tell you!" I say. "Even after the fact, you can't decide what to do."

I'm hoping this bit of logic will restore my parents' sanity, thus returning my albums to their rightful place in my bedroom. I look up with the begging eyes of a street urchin, but neither of them comes close to giving in, so I try a different tack. "You realize I'm going to lose my girlfriend, right? That being grounded for this long almost ensures she's going to break up with me and find someone else."

"She's welcome to come here and visit," my mother says.

"To do homework or help you with your chores," my father adds.

"An invitation no girl can refuse."

"Don't push it, Quinn." Mom checks her watch and heads inside for her three-o'clock call with Dr. Fredericks.

My father looks at me and shakes his head. "I'll be glad when she's out of this psychobabble phase," he says. "This is worse than the months of crystals and wheatgrass."

"What's so bad about wheatgrass?"

My father and I both whip around at the sound of Soosie's voice. When she hugs me, I notice she's put on probably fifteen pounds since we last saw her—not that I'd ever say anything. I want to live to see tomorrow, thank you very much.

"You've grown three inches." Soosie doesn't waste any time mangling my hair, giving me grief for how long it is.

Her hair is darker than usual, which I chalk off to spending less time in the sun. After I unload her stuff and watch her scarf down a turkey sandwich, she asks me about Brett. "Do you know where he's staying?" she asks. "Let's try to find him today."

I tell her I haven't seen him since the log cabin fiasco.

"I hope he hasn't turned himself in." She's pushed herself away from the counter and is pacing around the kitchen.

Mom screams when she finally emerges from the bedroom and finds Soosie standing in the kitchen. They cry, jump up and down—act so much like GIRLS that it actually makes me laugh. I'm relieved when Soosie pulls back her hair with a rubber band from the junk drawer and tells my mom all she wants to do is cook. Mom opens the door of the fridge, showing off the kale, tomatoes, scallions, ginger, and chicken she stocked up on anticipating Soosie's arrival. Dad goes to put on Miles Davis's *Kind of Blue*, but I run to the small stack of LPs Soosie brought with her and grab Creedence's *Cosmo's Factory* instead. My father puts the Miles Davis back with a laugh and I take my place at the sink to wash the vegetables. Besides my recent troubles, it's been a good year, but it doesn't really feel like home till just this moment when all four of us are together.

Mom sits on one of the stools watching Soosie prepare the chicken with lemon zest, salt, and pepper. "I have no idea where you got these skills. It's genetically impossible."

"My sister Ellie's a great cook," Dad says. "Maybe she got them from her."

I don't care where or why Soosie got her culinary

talent, as long as she keeps cranking out the meals while she's home.

When we sit outside to eat, I realize I should've invited Caroline to join us. I decide to run over after dinner and see if she wants to join us for dessert. (Homemade butterscotch pudding—count me in.)

Soosie's experiences in Boston, as well as the election in November, dominate much of the dinner conversation. Soosie also tells us about stopping in Joshua Tree on the drive back and the commune Melanie wanted to live in for a while. Every half hour or so, I jump up and turn over one of the records Soosie brought home. (It's not just the music I miss but the vinyl itself, the artwork on the covers, the liner notes—EVERYTHING.)

My mother gives one of her secret looks to my father, the same one she uses for early birthday presents or a surprise night at the drive-in. My father nods slightly, and suddenly what I've been dreaming about for weeks— getting my records back—seems like a reality.

I have never been so wrong.

"We wanted to wait till Soosie got home so we could tell you both together," Mom begins. "But your father and I have decided we need some space. We're going to separate for a while."

I look over at Soosie to see if she had any inkling about this bombshell, but she looks as surprised as I am.

"You said 'for a while,'" Soosie finally says. "So this isn't permanent."

"You're just trying it, right? Then you'll get back together?" My voice squeaks with a desperation that embarrasses me.

"This has been coming for several months," my father says. "We didn't want to say anything until we were sure."

"It sounds like you're *not* sure," Soosie says. "It sounds like a trial to me."

My mother reaches for my father's hand, more out of stability than romance. "We've talked about this a lot. We're not doing anything rash."

"Well, it certainly sounds that way," I say. "Oh, by the way, we've been married for more than twenty years and we just decided we don't love each other anymore."

"Nobody said that." My father seems almost angry at my comment. "Of course we love each other. We're trying to do this with respect and consideration. It's about two good people growing apart—nothing more than that."

"It is more than that!" I continue. "What am I supposed to do?"

My mother reaches for my hand, but I pull it away. "You can stay here, in your same room. I'm going to move into Ellen's while she's on tour—you'll have a room there too. I'll find my own place when she gets back."

"Or you might decide to move back here," Soosie says. "Right? That's a possibility too."

Neither of our parents answers.

"Right?" Soosie sounds even more desperate than I do, which is a small relief.

"Anything's a possibility," Dad finally answers.

"But not a probability," my mother adds.

"This isn't fair," Soosie says. "I just got home!"

"We wanted to tell you in person," Dad says. "Not over the phone."

"It's almost summer vacation!" I realize this has no bearing on the state of my parents' marriage, but I feel it's an important point anyway.

"This won't be easy for any of us," Mom says. "We all have to do the best we can."

Soosie stacks the dishes with so much force, I'm afraid they might break. "Whose idea was it? Who wanted the separation?"

My parents look at each other for the answer. It wasn't a question they anticipated.

"It was mine," my mother says. "But your father and I agree things haven't been right for a while."

The conversation has suddenly become more personal and intimate than I care to know about. Before my eyes, Soosie reverts to her ten-year-old self, her face crumpled with hurt and tears.

"So glad I came home! This was definitely worth it—thanks, guys!"

I follow her lead and head to my room down the hall, momentarily forgetting about Caroline and the butterscotch pudding. I've been so worried Caroline was going to break up with me this year, little did I know I'd need all those breakup songs I'd been compiling for a different reason. But even if I DID have my records, you can't really crank up "She's Leaving Home" when your mom's the one who's taking off. How do you prepare for something like this? Isn't it bad enough we have to deal with wildfires, smog, mudslides, and earthquakes? Do we have to deal with emotional disasters too?

I trip over the clean laundry my mother's placed in my room and kick the basket several times until it skids across the floor, exploding the clean clothes across my bed. My Gibson in its stand seems too perfect and erect; I get an urge to pick it up and smash it into a million pieces like Pete Townshend. The thought leaves as quickly as it came—I'm not a rock star with unlimited funds. Far from it. I'm a kid with pretty much nothing and a family that's splintering apart.

Almost as a way to apologize to my guitar, I take it off its stand and lie on the rug holding it, as if its very presence can ward off the emptiness. Besides this whole thing with my parents, my band just broke up, I'm grounded, and I've been worried my girlfriend's breaking up with me—I AM MENTALLY UNPREPARED FOR ALL THIS.

I stare up at the ceiling until it hits me like a ton of bricks: YOU'RE LOSING HER, SHE CAN'T STAY, SHE IS UNHAPPY. Jim, Janis, and Jimi weren't talking about Caroline; they were talking about my mom! Unlike Houdini, I *did* connect with souls from the other side, and they were RIGHT.

I hurry to Soosie's room, where my parents have stashed my albums and Ouija board. I grab the board and planchette, then race out to the yard. I look around for the trash can; it's at the end of the driveway waiting for tomorrow's pickup. I open the lid and jam the Ouija board and planchette deep inside.

My magic Ouija is gone, finished, history. Right along with my old definition of *family*.

feel like a sap for envying Ryan this year, as if tickets to the Lakers and new albums can make up for a giant wrecking ball swinging in and ruining your parents' marriage. I'm amazed at my own immaturity and shortsightedness, the same kid who also wanted to pretend his country wasn't at war.

This growing up thing is NO FUN. No fun at all.

FOR WHAT IT'S WORTH

5/72

When influential rock critic Nik Cohn wasn't thrilled with the rock opera <u>Tommy</u> the first time he heard it, Pete Townshend decided to make some changes to his main character. Since Cohn was a huge pinball aficionado, Townshend wrote "Pinball Wizard" and made Tommy a pinball whiz kid; Cohn subsequently gave the new album raves. If Townshend hadn't been sucking up to a critic, we'd have missed out on one of rock's greatest opening riffs.

Townshend's famous guitar smashing actually started as an accident, when he sent the head of his guitar through the ceiling at a performance at the Railway Tavern. Mad that people in the audience were laughing, he proceeded to smash the rest of the guitar onstage. The next week, a huge crowd showed up for the show and Townshend's been smashing guitars ever since.

As much as Mom swears our lives won't be any different, they are. Because Soosie works in the store, she gets to see Mom almost every day, while I end up practicing guitar in my room after school and shuttling between having dinner here with Dad and meeting Mom at Cass's house with a duffel bag full of clothes and my toothbrush. I keep hoping that when Cass returns, Mom will come back home, but after I see the ads for bungalows she circled in the classifieds, it begins to sink in that her move might be permanent.

Dad doesn't stay late at work anymore; he comes straight home and tries to be cheerful as he makes us spaghetti or grills some steaks. I know he's trying to be strong on my account, because some nights when I can't sleep, I sneak out to the garage and watch him from the window. He still rebuilds his amps, but he's unfocused and often just stares at the tubes while listening to John Coltrane. I think about going in to comfort him but know it'll just end with the two of us in tears. That might be a good thing, but I'm not able to handle that yet, maybe never.

Mom tries to make Cass's house seem like home by lighting the same candles and playing the same music she did at our house, but it feels like we're guests here and we both know it. She takes me to see *Jeremiah Johnson* at the movies, which is something she never would've done before. (I don't complain, however, because it wordlessly brings my being grounded to a wheezing halt.) I feel like I'm leading Ryan's life, not mine, but try not to make things worse by griping. Mom sits on the edge of my bed like she used to do when I was little and doesn't leave till I tell her I have to sleep. She says she's happy, but to me it always seems like she's just about to cry.

When Caroline gets back from visiting San Diego with her parents, I tell her the news. She's so surprised, she makes us late for class with all her questions. She passes me notes throughout art class until I finally write back that I'll tell her everything after school.

As we walk home, I tell her about my mother staying at Cass's, how upset Soosie is, how quiet my father's been. When I tell her I threw away the Ouija board, she seems almost relieved.

"I'm glad you got rid of it. You were relying on it too much."

"We had access to Club 27—who wouldn't use it every day? Besides, they were right about Mom leaving, when all along—" I realize where the end of the sentence is going and slam on the brakes. Unfortunately, my super-smart girlfriend is way ahead of me.

"Club 27 told you she was leaving, but what?"

I can't dig up anything that makes a shred of sense, so don't say a word.

"You thought I was the one leaving, right?" She spins around to face me as she walks. "Is that why you haven't trusted me—because you thought Club 27 told you not to?"

When you put it under a microscope like that, it sounds a bit ridiculous, but at the time it made perfect sense to me.

Caroline looks as if she's formulating her thoughts before she speaks—a nice trick I might want to try sometime. "I know what Lynne said to you after she and Tom came over the first time."

"You do?"

"She told me afterward because she felt bad."

"Then why did she say it?"

"To cause trouble, to have a laugh?" She looks me squarely in the eyes. "Knowing you, Quinn, some stupid comment might make you totally paranoid and send you running to the Ouija board for answers."

My girlfriend knows me better than I thought. "I wouldn't do that," I lie.

"I can't come up with any other reason why you don't trust me."

As we reach my house, I try to change the subject but Caroline will have none of it.

"Every time I invite a friend over or hang out with someone else, you make me feel like a criminal. It's not cool."

I debate mentioning the fact that the someone in question is none other than my best friend, Ryan. But I don't say anything because as Caroline's talking, my brain is fixated on one question and one question only: IS SHE BREAKING UP WITH ME NOW? The ever-present turntable in my head cues up Al Green's "Let's Stay Together."

"Quinn? Say something!"

Telling her I've been in my own weird world for the last few moments while she's trying to have a heart-to-heart talk is tantamount to signing my own death warrant, so I dig deep down and come up with some truths of my own.

"I'm sorry. It was stupid. Just please don't break up with me."

The gods must feel sorry for this poor kid trying to

save his first relationship and decide to take pity, because suddenly Caroline smiles. "Of course I'm not breaking up with you! Did you not hear a word I just said?"

This is the price for paying more attention to the thoughts running through your own cobwebbed head instead of listening to what somebody right in front of you is actually saying. I pull her toward me for a kiss and promise her I'll stop being such an imbecile. I mean, she's right—I HAVE spent as much time worried about losing her as I have just being her boyfriend. She's my first girlfriend and no one offered me a training manual, so I've been winging it, too embarrassed to ask Ryan or even my parents for advice, instead running my half-baked questions by a group of rock star ghosts. If I'm going to stay in this relationship, I better get my act together.

"Is this the Caroline I've heard so much about?" Soosie bounds into the room and gives Caroline a giant hug. She's been staying on and off with friends to avoid being home, but I finally talked her into coming by tonight to meet Caroline. For once, Soosie's timing is perfect, saving me from any more relationship talk. She's going on a buying trip for Mom's store tomorrow and solicits ideas from Caroline as to what kind of things she should be looking out for. While they yak about fabrics and scarves, I work on some transcriptions for Frank.

"Come on," Soosie orders. "Let's look for Brett again."

I tell her that since the fire, I've looked everywhere, but he's nowhere to be found.

"I heard the cops combed the woods," Soosie says. "But I'm not giving up till we find him or they do."

Caroline and I climb into the orange van and head down to Sunset with Soosie. We check out the Guitar Center, the Whisky, the Roxy. We go down Santa Monica Boulevard and drive by the Troubadour and Barney's Beanery. We cruise the side streets, we drive up to Mulholland—nothing. When we get to the intersection where the cabin is, we spot a cop in his car outside the fence.

"Like they don't have anything better to do," Soosie says.

"Maybe they gave up on Brett and are here for another reason," Caroline suggests.

If I had said it, Soosie would've jumped down my throat, but because it was Caroline's comment, she lets it slide. I can tell she's upset by the time we pull into the driveway, so I suggest Caroline and I help her cook, knowing chopping vegetables and herbs is the number one way to make Soosie feel better. She takes me up on my offer and the three of us make a big bowl of gazpacho that we eat on the front porch.

"Your sister is the *best*," Caroline says later.

"She's actually more like a beast."

But Caroline can't be persuaded otherwise and gushes on about Soosie until I grab my guitar and start playing.

I ask Caroline if she has any requests, secretly hoping she'll say Santana so I can show off some of my improved riffs. Instead she asks for Carly Simon. (PS— you know I play GUITAR, right? Not sit at a piano singing chick songs?)

But I play "Anticipation" anyway, happy I'm not grounded anymore and can spend a Saturday night with my girlfriend. Staying on the same theme of expectation, I launch into "Waiting" by Santana for my own enjoyment. After Caroline leaves, I play for a few more hours, hoping Brett has finally found his way to somewhere safe.

I know it doesn't make any sense, but for some reason my parents splitting up and Brett going missing are inexplicably linked in my mind. It's as if finding Brett and solving his problems with the draft board could create some kind of domino effect that would eventually cause my parents to get back together. Illogical, yes, but what do you expect from a fourteen-year-old going through major music withdrawal?

FOR WHAT IT'S WORTH

6/72

Carlos Santana washed dishes and
played guitar on the streets for spare
change in San Francisco before his life
radically changed one Sunday
afternoon. Promoter Bill Graham used to
run matinees at the Fillmore, where he
showcased three acts for a dollar. When
Paul Butterfield showed up barefoot and
wasted for his set, Graham assembled
some musicians from the audience, guys

from the Dead, Jefferson Airplane, as well as Michael Bloomfield, who was supposed to play with Butterfield. They needed a guitarist, and Santana's roommate told them he knew a "skinny Mexican kid" who could really play. Bloomfield said okay, Santana went from audience member to bandmate, and proceeded to blow everyone away with his emotional guitar solos. He started forming a band the next day.

As I pass the newsstand on Santa Monica, a man scanning the magazines takes a step back, blocking my path. I start to walk around him but am frozen in my steps because the guy standing in front of me is Brett.

"I'm sorry if I got you in trouble with the police." He pulls a magazine from the rack and thumbs through it as he talks.

"I'm the one who caused YOU trouble," I say. "It was stupid of me to go to the cabin, never mind invite my friends." I look from side to side to make sure no policemen are around.

I tell him Soosie is back from Boston and has spent the past several days looking for him. "She's selling her van to get you some money. She's got a guy coming to look at it in a few days."

"Tell her not to. I'm turning myself in today—I can't take it anymore."

"You've been here for months. Can't you hold out a little longer?"

"I'm living like a prisoner anyway, an inch away from a nervous breakdown. I have to turn myself in so I can sleep."

I'm shocked by how much older Brett seems than the first time I saw him. It looks like he hasn't slept or showered in weeks.

He gazes over my shoulder to make sure no one's walking toward us. "If I'd gone to college or lied to the draft board and told them I was a homosexual, I wouldn't have to deal with any of this. Instead I'm going to be sitting in a jail cell or traveling thousands of miles to a country on the other side of the world trying to kill people I've never met. It's not really what I had in mind when I turned nineteen."

The man who runs the newsstand is just a few feet away, rearranging newspapers. He's probably waiting to see if we'll buy anything, but his presence gives us both the creeps, so Brett and I start walking.

The last thing I ever thought I'd be doing is giving some older kid advice on the war, but my mom is right—like it or not, the war has affected me and I can't hide my head in the sand anymore.

"I know you feel like you're abandoning your country, but sitting in jail for the next few years is just as much of a waste as the war is. You should leave."

"I can't afford to," he says. "Can't even afford to hitchhike home. I'm turning myself into the marine office on Melrose after saying goodbye to some friends. Is Soosie around?"

I tell him she and Tanya went on a buying trip for the store and won't be back for a few days. I beg him to wait, but he says he can't.

"Good luck, Quinn. I hope this war and the draft are over before you're my age. I'd hate to see a good kid like you go through this too. Give my parents a call—they'll know where I end up. You guys come visit me, okay?"

The thought of Soosie and me going through prison metal detectors and talking to Brett on battered old telephones while he sits behind a wall of glass seems ludicrous, like out of a movie. I didn't think it was possible to feel any worse, but as I climb the cement steps to school, I do.

Ryan grabs me in the hall to talk about the eponymous Eagles album finally being released, the kind of conversation I usually look forward to. But all I can think about is the decision Brett made today, based on laws and rules he didn't have a say in.

Mr. Woodrow looks at his watch as we take our seats. "Let's start off with another photograph," he says. "This one ran in almost every newspaper in the country this week. It was taken by AP photographer Nick Ut in a small village in South Vietnam." This time, he doesn't hand out one photograph for us to pass around; he's made crisp copies. When the stack of photos gets to me, I'm too flabbergasted to pass along the rest. It's an image of a group of young Vietnamese children, running down the street screaming, surrounded by smoke and military men. One of the girls is naked and crying.

"A South Vietnamese pilot mistook these civilians and soldiers for the enemy and bombed them with napalm. The little girl in the center tore off her clothes and was yelling 'too hot, too hot' in her native language."

Many of my classmates turn the photos over on their desks to spare themselves the horrific image. I, on the other hand, am transfixed. It's the expression of panic, fear, and confusion on the girl's face as she literally runs for her life. I look over to Caroline, who's as shocked as I am. She doesn't even care that her eyes are brimming with tears.

"This isn't fair!" she shouts. "How old is this girl— eleven?"

"Nine," Woodrow answers.

Ryan and Willy shove the page into their note-books, already onto the next thing. Not me, not this time. The photo has split open a part of me I didn't even know was closed. Woodrow lectures about a "picture being worth a thousand words," how he hopes this photograph gets people furious enough to do something about the war. Maybe Caroline's passion for album covers and photographs has rubbed off on me, maybe the images of girls screaming over dead bodies and running from napalm attacks have finally gotten through where words didn't. This photographer thousands of miles away has made me realize with 100 percent certainty that Brett can't spend the next few years in jail for opposing something as terrible and wrong as this war.

When the bell rings, Caroline races to my desk. "Suppose my brother was in that village? He could've gotten killed! Is this the kind of thing he has to witness every day?"

I nod but am busy formulating questions of my own. "Can you cover for me? Tell anyone who asks that I went home sick."

"*Are* you sick?" she asks.

"To my stomach." I grab my books and sneak out the side door.

When I get home twenty minutes later, I'm surprised to find both my parents at the house, paying bills.

"You okay?" my mother asks, always on alert. "What's wrong?"

"THIS is what's wrong." I take the copy of the photo and place it between them on the table.

"Where did you get this?" my father asks. "This is horrible."

"It happened in Vietnam. It's in all the papers."

My father hurries down to the driveway and returns with the *Los Angeles Times*.

My mother's hand covers her mouth and she shakes her head when she sees the photo, now official. "These are children. This is criminal!"

It dawns on my father that I'm not at school. "Did you come home to show us this?"

"No, I came home to get my records."

My parents look confused.

"You want to listen to music at a time like this?" my mother asks. "They're still confiscated, remember?"

AS IF I COULD FORGET. I walk into Soosie's room and stare at the crates of my prized possessions. "Can you give me a ride to the record store?"

"Now?" my father asks. "Can't this wait?"

"You're upset by the photograph—understandably," my mother adds. "Let me drive you back to school."

My father must recognize the determination in my eyes because he holds his hand out to stop my mother and asks what I'm planning to do.

I hoist up the first crate and balance it on my hips. "Sell every last one of these records."

My mother still doesn't get it. "I don't see how selling your albums will help these poor children. What's going on, Quinn?"

"Maybe I can't do much, but I can do SOMETHING." Before the sentence is out of my mouth, my father grabs his keys and helps me load the car.

Drastic? Impulsive?

   Maybe.

But have you seen that picture? Go find it in your local newspaper or look it up at the library, then tell me you wouldn't do everything in your power to make sure something like that never happens again.

FOR WHAT IT'S WORTH

6/72

Many of you know Glenn Frey, Don
Henley, Bernie Leadon, and Randy
Meisner from playing around town, most
notably as Linda Ronstadt's backup
band. (I know a lot of you went to her
show at Disneyland last year mostly to
see them.) Well, they just formed their
own band, and their debut album,
Eagles, just hit the stores. (They're
called Eagles, not THE Eagles--get it

right.) Now, critics can't stop talking
about "Southern California country
rock," but for those of us who live
here, it's nothing new. Bernie Leadon
played with ex-Byrds members Gram
Parsons and Chris Hillman in the
Flying Burrito Brothers, a country rock
band if there ever was one. Randy
Meisner was in Poco, another country-
based band from L.A. Not to mention the
country sound in the Byrds' <u>Sweetheart
of the Rodeo</u>. The critics can pretend
this whole phenomenon is a hot trend,
but anyone who's been listening to the
music coming out of the Canyon these
past several years knows there's
nothing new about it at all.

At the record store, Jeff and my father help me unload the car.

"Are you *sure* about this?" Jeff says. "It's taken you years to build this collection."

No one knows that better than I do.

"You won't get retail," he continues. "I can only give you a percentage of what you paid new. You want to think about it for a few days?"

I tell him I need the money today and bring in another crate. Even Terry, the music snob who almost never gives me the time of day when I come in, eyes my collection with interest. I take special pride when he slides the vinyl out of the sleeve of *Alone Together*. "You sure you want to trade this one in?" he asks.

I'd be lying if I didn't admit that I hesitated a few

moments before keeping that album in the pile. Terry nonchalantly slips the album behind the counter, probably to keep for himself.

"This one too?" he asks.

I say goodbye to *GWW*, the best of the Dylan bootlegs. "It's all yours—as long as you pay me for it."

While Jeff adds up my total trade-in, my father hangs around the blues section eyeing a John Lee Hooker album with envy.

"You want to get it?" I ask. "We'll have enough credit."

"No, that money's going to a good cause. I'll get this another time."

After running the numbers through the adding machine he keeps underneath the counter, Jeff hands me a long strip of paper. "Three hundred twenty-two dollars. Seem right to you?"

I have never once thought of selling my collection, have no idea what all of this music is worth. But $322 is more money than I've ever had my hands on and is certainly enough to get Brett over the Canadian border. I tell Jeff okay and he runs to the bank a few doors down to get some cash. When he comes back, he counts the twenties into a large stack in my outstretched hands.

"You want a few moments alone with your albums?" Jeff asks solemnly.

Most people might think he's kidding, but Jeff's as

dead serious about his music as I am. He knows a giant chunk of my soul sits on that Formica counter and he has enough respect for me as a fellow devotee to offer me a few minutes alone to grieve.

My father doesn't rush me as I slowly flip through my albums one last time. Donovan, Badfinger, Harry Nilsson, the Stooges, Plastic Ono Band, Quicksilver Messenger Service, James Gang, Nazz, Jethro Tull, America, Grand Funk Railroad, Joan Baez, Genesis, Yes, Firesign Theater, Cheech & Chong, R.E.O. Speedwagon, Mott the Hoople, Mountain, McCartney, Santana, Black Sabbath, Monty Python, Elton John, Cat Stevens, James Taylor, and so many others. It's like saying goodbye to friends I know intimately.

After chiding myself for not making more cassette tapes, dozens of questions fill my head: How long will it take me to build a new collection? Will Ryan and Willy let me borrow some of theirs in the meantime? Will I survive by listening to Dad's blues, jazz, and country records? Will I still be able to play guitar without all these album covers staring back at me? CAN I FUNCTION IN THE WORLD WITHOUT THIS WALL OF SOUND?

But I don't have time to sit around philosophizing; I've got to hurry to the induction center before Brett turns himself in.

As Dad pulls the car onto Melrose, I remind myself to tell Soosie how wrong she was about our father. (I won't need much reminding; one of my favorite things on the planet is letting Soosie know when she's wrong.) Dad's chomping at the bit at the red light, barely waiting till it turns green before hitting the gas. Just because he fought in Korea doesn't mean he's some war-mongering soldier out to make sure every last kid serves his country too.

"Is it because you're against the war?" I ask. "Is that why you dropped everything to help me today?"

He turns the radio down. "It's not that at all. I'm your dad—it's my job to support you."

I try to follow that thread of logic. "So if I was racing to turn Brett in, you'd drive me there too?"

He smiles. "In that case, I might've let you walk."

I point to a spot up ahead and Dad parallel parks the station wagon.

"Why were you and Mom home today? Are you thinking of getting back together?"

He hands me several coins to put in the meter and says that he and Mom were discussing stuff like mortgage payments.

"You shouldn't pin your hopes on your mom moving back in. We both love you very much—I'm just afraid we have to do it separately right now."

After seeing that photo in Woodrow's class, my parents' living situation has moved down a few rungs on the life and death ladder. Instead of worrying about their relationship for a change, I concentrate on how we're going to find Brett.

Dad suggests he go in first to see if he can find out any information about Brett without mentioning his name. I'm glad Dad volunteered. With my luck, I'd end up divulging some piece of critical information that would get Brett into even MORE trouble. While he's inside, I flip through the wad of cash in my pocket, all the while telling myself not to get too attached.

Fifteen minutes later, my father exits the building. "I chatted up the colonel on duty. It's been a pretty slow morning so far, which means Brett hasn't made it here yet. Any idea where he might be?"

The log cabin? The woods? The newsstand? But I don't have to guess because I recognize the figure with the hooded sweatshirt from a block away. I hurry toward Brett before he gets to the induction center. He seems shocked when I introduce him to my dad.

"We're here to stop you," I explain. "To talk you into hitting the road instead."

I hand him the wad of bills. "It's three hundred twenty-two dollars, hopefully enough to get to Vancouver."

The way Brett gazes at the money makes me think he's never held this much cash before either.

"I can't take this," he says. "I don't know when I'll be able to pay you back."

"I don't want it back." I smooth out the folded copy

of the photo and hand it to him. "I just don't want anything like this to happen again."

"I saw this today," Brett says. "I couldn't decide if I should cry or be angry."

"I got angry."

My dad suggests the man who took the photograph was probably hoping for just that response. He also reaches into the pocket of his workpants and takes out a wad of folded bills. "Take this too. Between this and Quinn's, you should be okay till you find a job up there."

How has my father gone from being awarded the Bronze Star in Korea to helping a draft dodger escape to Canada? It makes me wonder what's changed more—him or war itself.

"Shhh—do you hear that?" I ask.

My father and Brett freeze when they hear the sirens.

Three police cars suddenly screech to the curb in front of the induction center as two soldiers in khaki uniforms hurry out of the building. The three of us are a block away but hold our breath.

"What do you think I should do, sir?" Brett asks.

The fact that Brett just called my father sir makes me realize how incredibly difficult this whole desertion thing must be for him.

Dad doesn't hesitate, doesn't blink. "I think you should go. Run."

It's almost as if Brett has been waiting for someone

to say just that. He draws me in for an awkward hug. "Tell Soosie goodbye for me. Tell her I couldn't wait another day."

I tell him I will, then look over at the cop cars and soldiers a few yards away. "Go!"

"It might take me years, but I'll pay you back."

I want to tell him it's unnecessary, but he's already half a block west and can't hear me. My father's eyes are riveted on the men in uniform hurrying inside the building. He whips around to see if Brett is safely gone, then shoots his arm up into the air in an unmistakable peace sign. It's a gesture I've seen a million times but never by this ex-soldier, this man in greasy workpants, struggling to do the right thing. My father holds his arm high, unwavering against the clouds. It's the closest I've felt to my dad in years.

We walk a few moments in silence. "That was very generous," Dad says, "but you know it doesn't guarantee anything. Brett is still wanted by the authorities, the war is still raging, children will still die. . . ." His voice trails off as he gathers the strength to finish. "Your mother and I are still going our separate ways, no matter how many heroic deeds you do, no matter how good a kid you are."

It's almost as if my father has been reading my mind these last several weeks. "I know I can't change any of that," I finally answer. "It was just a gesture to make things a little better, that's all."

"It's all you can do sometimes—just improve one thing." He says this in his bad Johnny Carson voice, but I laugh anyway, knowing how hard it was for my dad to even broach this conversation today.

My father spots a meter maid a few cars behind ours so we sprint back to the station wagon. She gives us a "lucky you" smile as we pull away from our expired meter.

It's a pretty good day for beating the system.

Has it sunk in yet?

Will the black hole left by my album collection slowly suck my soul into the emptiness?

Have I made a GIANT mistake?

I pull out the atlas, find the west coast of the United States, and trace my finger up through the mountains and the valleys, along the Pacific Ocean. Past San Luis Obispo, Carmel, San Francisco, Mendocino, into Oregon, over the Columbia River, to Seattle and the Canadian border. My finger hovers over the dark blue line separating the U.S. from Canada, an arbitrary border dividing the lives of thousands of Americans into criminal or free. All I can do is hope Brett becomes the latter.

FOR WHAT IT'S WORTH

6/72

Harry Nilsson worked the night shift at
a bank in the Valley while he wrote
dozens of songs and shopped them
around town. When he started selling
them after years of writing, he finally
earned enough money to quit his job.
He's one of the Beatles' favorite
American performers, even if two of the
giant hits--"Coconut" and "Jump into the
Fire"--consist of one chord and one

chord only. Coincidentally, he wrote a song called "One," which was covered by Three Dog Night on their debut album and was a giant smash too. Nilsson upped the ante on that one, though, using seven pretty difficult chords, or at least they're pretty difficult for me.

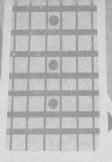

The First Albums I'm Going to Buy When I Get Some Money Again

★ **Roxy Music**—Roxy Music

★ **Honky Château**—Elton John

★ **Eat a Peach**—The Allman Brothers Band

★ **Pink Moon**—Nick Drake

★ **Burgers**—Hot Tuna

★ **Just Another Band From L.A.**—Frank Zappa and the Mothers

★ **Manassas**—Stephen Stills and Manassas

★ **Exile on Main St.**—The Rolling Stones

★ **Live at Max's Kansas City**—Velvet Underground

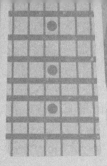

★ **Jeff Beck Group**—Jeff Beck

★ **Tea for the Tillerman**—Cat Stevens

★ **Mud Slide Slim and the Blue Horizon**—James Taylor

★ **Last of the Red Hot Burritos**—The Flying Burrito Brothers

★ **Eagles**—Eagles

When Soosie comes home a few days later and realizes she missed Brett, she's furious. Only after Dad and I convince her that Brett was literally about to crack from the pressure does she stop yelling and collapse on her bed in tears. My dad holds her in his arms and lets her cry like a baby.

"It's so unfair," she says. "It never should've come to this."

I tell her as soon as the war's over, Brett will be back in this country as good as new.

"He'll still be a criminal," she says slowly. "The only way he and every other draft dodger can return is by presidential pardon."

I look over at my dad to see if this is true. For some reason, I thought once the war ended, it would be like someone called *olly, olly, oxen free*, and all the guys who didn't want to go to war could finally come back home.

"That's not the way it works," Dad says. "Brett and tens of thousands of other guys committed a crime. That doesn't go away."

After a while Soosie jumps up and wipes her cheeks. "Did you say you sold your records? Are you *kidding*?" She puts her hand to my forehead as if I have a fever. "Oh my God, how are you *coping*?"

I yank her hand off me like it's contaminated, then bring up the question at hand: if the guy coming over tonight buys her van, maybe she'd like to reimburse me SO I CAN GET SOME OF MY ALBUMS BACK.

"I would, Quinnie, but he already called to say he's not interested."

When I tell Caroline I sold my entire collection to help Brett, she doesn't believe me until I show her the cavernous space in my room where my records used to be. Because the milk crates covered the hardwood floors all these years, the wood underneath's a darker color than in the rest of the room. The only items in the empty space now are my guitar, amp, and the photo of the girl in Vietnam running from the napalm.

Caroline looks at the Vietnam photo for a long time. "Can you imagine taking a picture like this while something so horrible is happening right in front of you? Most people's instincts would be to run for your life or get help—not to focus your camera and shoot." She sits down slowly on the bed, still holding the photo. "I'm not sure anymore if I have what it takes to be a news photographer."

I sit down next to her. "Woodrow was right about this photograph—it will infuriate people and help put an end to this stupid war. Nick Ut made a difference." Caroline looks about to cry, so I put my arm around her. (Is she impressed I remembered the photographer's name?) "Besides, after he snapped this picture, he took these kids to the hospital."

She wipes her eyes. "He did? How do you know?"

Even though I'm embarrassed to admit it, I tell her I stayed after class with Woodrow a few days ago and asked him to tell me everything he knew about the photograph. "He brought me down to the school library and helped me find several newspaper articles. He was pretty helpful."

"I keep thinking about my brother," Caroline says. "I'm proud he's serving our country but I hope the war ends soon. I feel like there's a bomb hidden in our house just waiting to go off. Every time there's a knock at the front door, my mother bursts into tears. Billy being gone has changed everything."

Talking about the war makes me wonder how Brett is doing and if he's okay.

Caroline peeks out the curtain to the end of the

driveway. "Your mom's here, and your dad's screaming—that can't be good."

I head outside to check. Fighting in front of the neighbors would be a new low, not something either parent would be proud of. Thankfully, it's not their relationship that has my father enraged but the front page of the newspaper. I scan the article he's shoved into my hands.

"A break-in at a hotel in Washington, DC? I don't get it," I say.

"It's just the beginning," my father says. "The tip of the iceberg."

"We don't know that yet," my mother says. "It could be a coincidence."

"The office that was broken into belonged to the Democratic National Committee—just the way Daniel Ellsberg's psychiatrist's office got broken into after he published the Pentagon Papers!" I'm not sure I've ever seen my father so mad. "What is happening to this country? Who's in charge?"

I stare at the trash can where I tossed my Ouija board a few weeks ago and for the first time since, feel its supernatural pull. This was the kind of question I used to pose to Jimi, Janis, and Jim, but I take Caroline's advice and make up my own mind for a change. I borrow the paper from my dad and head back to my room to read the rest of the article.

"Woodrow's going to go nuts," Caroline says as she reads along with me.

When we get to school, Woodrow is nuts times a hundred. They're now calling this whole thing Watergate because the break-in happened at the Watergate Hotel. "You just watch," Woodrow says. "There's a huge conspiracy underneath this. Heads are going to roll." He must've also ranted in the teachers' lounge or some students complained because Principal Munroe pulls him out of the classroom and tells him to "take it down a notch." Woodrow can't, of course, but there's only a few days left of school, so Munroe doesn't have any leverage. We spend the rest of the class time before vacation writing letters to our senators as Woodrow paces the aisles between our desks in a nonstop tirade about Nixon, Cambodia, and the upcoming election. I hate to admit it, but I'm really going to miss Mr. Woodrow next year.

When I take the mail in at home, I notice one of the letters is addressed to me. The only mail I've ever received is from Soosie at college or my aunt Tamara, so I open the envelope quickly.

Dear Quinn,
I just wanted to let you know that thanks to you I'm safely in Vancouver. After all my anxiety, I crossed the border easily—in the trunk of a car driven by two sympathetic nuns. Vancouver is a beautiful city with a

great waterfront and nice people. I got a job at a sandwich shop near my apartment and I'm taking a night class too. For the first time in a while, I feel safe and that's because of you and your father. I want to send you money as I get it—I still can't believe you made such a sacrifice for a relative stranger. Write back and let me know how you're doing.

Sincerely,

Brett Marshall

It dawns on me that I never even knew Brett's last name until now.

Inside the envelope is a twenty-dollar bill, which I immediately shove into the pocket of my jeans. Ryan is leaving tonight for his annual trip to the Berkshires; I call him to meet me at the record store before he goes.

I haven't mentally prepared myself for the fact that some of the records filling the bins used to be mine.

"You going to buy back your own?" Ryan asks. "Or start off fresh with some new ones?"

He's wearing a white button-down shirt that his mom made him put on for the plane ride. The fact that he's leaving for almost two months makes me incredibly sad.

Jeff interrupts to tell us about some of the new stuff that came in Tuesday—a Bob Marley import!—as well as some bootlegs he took in on trade. I can feel the twenty-dollar bill in my pocket squirming to get out, but I also want to spend some time with Ryan before he has to go.

We make small talk about his cousins, the time difference, how he won't see his father till September.

"Speaking of which, how's it going?" he asks.

He doesn't have to elaborate—I know what he's talking about.

"As well as can be expected, I guess," I answer. "I never thought my parents would separate."

"Join the club." He flips through the Beatles section, which takes up one whole segment of the bin. "Then when they get divorced, it's another whole thing. So final."

As if I haven't been dreading that too. I steer us away from this incredibly painful topic. "I spent so much time worried about Caroline leaving and it's my mother who hits the road. Ironic, huh?"

"Caroline *did* almost break up with you," he says. "But I talked her out of it."

THIS IS NEWS TO ME. I ask him to elaborate.

"Because you kept thinking she was cheating on you—and she wasn't. Girls hate it when you don't trust them."

I suddenly am transported back to my conversation with Caroline a few weeks ago. Is THIS what she was trying to tell me? "You talked her out of breaking up with me?"

"Yeah, and all the time you were thinking I was

going to steal her away. Talk about ironic. I wouldn't do that to you, Quinn."

I've known Ryan almost my whole life—his chewed-up nails and few random mustache hairs are as familiar to me as if they were my own.

"The person I should've trusted was you," I say. "I'm sorry I didn't."

"I'm glad she listened to me. Between that and your parents, your summer would've *sucked*."

Ain't that the truth.

"You may not like it, but you have to trust your parents too," Ryan continues.

"What is this, your big going-away speech? When did you get so smart all of a sudden?"

"I had to grow up pretty fast this year," he says. "It's not like I wanted to."

Jeff, thankfully, breaks up the conversation before Ryan and I start bawling. He holds up *Zeppelin IV* and *L.A. Woman*. "They're your old copies," Jeff says. "I can let you have them at a discount because the last owner took such good care of them."

"Their last owner was a *moron*," Ryan says. "With the worst taste in music in town."

"Like that stopped you from borrowing every record I ever owned," I reply, grateful that Ryan has returned us to our old teasing selves.

"Better hold on tight to that rock and roll," Jeff adds

on our way out. "There's an English disco opening on the Strip in a few months. Glam rock is making its way to Southern California."

Ryan and I walk back home trying to decide if this is bad news or not. (Bowie, T. Rex, Mott the Hoople—good. Glitter, jumpsuits, and eye makeup for guys—bad.) We argue about music the whole way back to our neighborhood. Why does Jethro Tull's *Thick as a Brick* have just one song? Couldn't they have broken up forty-four minutes of music into better chunks than that? And what does Chicago's "25 or 6 to 4" mean? Are they looking at a clock and wondering if it's 3:35 or 3:34? Or is it some kind of drunken code? And when Todd sings *"it wouldn't have made any difference if you loved me,"* is he saying "I don't care whether you loved me or not" or "if you really loved me, you wouldn't care about how I just screwed up?" And why do the Band's songs sound like there were written a hundred years ago in the Deep South, when they were actually penned by Robbie Robertson—a Canadian—just a few years ago? THESE are the kinds of questions that should be pondered for hours, especially walking up Laurel Canyon on a sunny summer afternoon with your best friend in the whole entire world.

"Maybe we can start another band in September," I suggest. "Start from scratch."

Ryan shields his eyes from the sun. "I'm not ruling

it out, but it was much more work than I thought it would be."

When we get to Ryan's street, he asks if I still have the Cap'n Crunch whistle. I tell him I tried to give it to Brett, but he was adamant about not breaking the law.

"A draft dodger who won't rip off the phone company— there's an oxymoron in there somewhere."

"So you WERE paying attention in Woodrow's class."

"Very funny. Call me, okay?" He takes a pen from his back pocket and writes his cousin's phone number on my hand.

When I wave goodbye to Ryan for the summer, the numbers on my hand flutter in the wind.

Does it make me a bad person if a tiny, infinitesimal part of me is still worried that something might have happened between Ryan and Caroline while I was grounded? Am I paranoid? Insane?

SEE WHAT HAPPENS WHEN YOU TAKE A GUY'S ALBUMS AWAY? HE LOSES HIS MIND.

FOR WHAT IT'S WORTH

6/72

On his first solo effort, Something/
Anything?, Todd Rundgren wrote, sang,
engineered, produced, and played every
instrument on three of the
breakthrough double album's four sides.
His song "Hello, It's Me" went to #5 on
Billboard; "I Saw the Light," #16. The
single "Couldn't I Just Tell You" is
influencing scores of other power pop
songs as we speak.

Rock's new wunderkind is producing other albums too--most notably The Band's Stage Fright and Badfinger's smash Straight Up. Not bad for a guy who just turned 24.

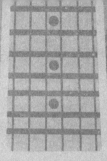

Songs That Make Me Feel Like Maybe I'll Get Through All This

★ "Across the Universe"—The Beatles

★ "Changes"—David Bowie

★ "The Times They Are A-Changing"—Bob Dylan

★ "Turn, Turn, Turn"—Pete Seeger

★ "New Morning"—Bob Dylan

★ "Getting Better"—The Beatles

★ "A Change Is Gonna Come"—Sam Cooke

★ "Beginnings"—Chicago

★ "Peaches en Regalia"—Frank Zappa

★ "Hey Jude"—The Beatles

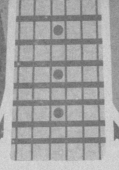

★ **"I Just Want to Celebrate"**—Rare Earth

★ **"Dust in the Wind"**—Todd Rundgren

★ **"Morning Has Broken"**—Cat Stevens

★ **"You Can't Always Get What You Want"**
—The Rolling Stones

Caroline has a job as an assistant in a photo lab for the summer, so I mostly see her on weekends. I take as many hours as I can get helping Dad at the dealership and housesitting around the neighborhood to try and save up enough cash to rebuild my record collection. Smog has socked in the city; it's already ninety degrees. What started out to be MY FIRST SUMMER WITH A GIRL-FRIEND is turning out to be a giant snooze.

With all the drama around Brett leaving, I never got to submit my list of the best albums of all time to the school paper. Patty was bummed—she'd been saving a full page for it and had to scramble to find a replacement piece. Sure, I could've thrown a list together in two seconds, but that's not how I do things, at least not where music is concerned. Since I have lots of time on my hands, I hone the list and tack it to the wall above my desk. I may not have any albums, but at least I have a list of my favorites.

I stop by the Canyon Store for a soda and take my time walking home. When I finally get there, I'm shocked to see Frank Zappa sitting on my front porch. I try to remember if I have any transcriptions due.

"I still have a few weeks for this new batch," I blurt out. "Is that okay?"

It takes Frank a few minutes to realize what I'm talking about. "Sure. No hurry. I'm here for a different reason."

I knew sooner or later word would get back to him about the incident at the log cabin. "It was a stupid mistake," I begin. "I never should've had a séance at your old house."

"The cabin?" Frank asks. "People go there all the time—the landlord needs to do a better job of keeping people out." He seems amused. "Séance, huh? Tell me more."

I tell him the story of Brett's unscheduled visit and how everyone thought he was Morrison's ghost.

"Sounds like you had about as much luck as Houdini had." I can't believe one of the hardest-working guys in the music business has nothing better to do than hang out on my porch and talk about one of the worst nights of my life.

"The door was open," he says after a few minutes. "I left you something inside."

I hurry into the house and almost stumble on a dozen large boxes. Of RECORDS!

"I had a lot of doubles, a lot of demos. Thought you might like to hear some of them."

I flip through the first box; I recognize a few of the album covers, but most are new to me. Frank stops when I get to one of his favorites. "*The Complete Works of Edgard Varèse, Volume One*," he says. "He blew my mind open when I was your age. I have several copies of this one—it's a classic. I bet I've listened to it five thousand times." I put the record on the turntable and Zappa leans back on one of the kitchen stools like he's gearing up for a treat.

The song I put on is called "Ionisation"; it's an instrumental with lots of percussion and cowbells, chimes, sirens, hammers, and triangles. I'm not sure if it's technically considered a song because it's so off-kilter and weird. The music is chaotic and strange and melodic and I immediately love it. (And not just because Frank is sitting right here.)

I wait a few moments before responding. "I can see what an influence this had on you—he uses a lot of the same techniques."

"Good luck transcribing that one." He goes through

the boxes and pulls several other records for me to check out later. "The music you listen to on the radio—it's fine. But you need to explore some of the stuff that doesn't make *Billboard*."

I stare at the boxes of records. These albums and 45s are a gold mine, Frank Zappa's personal collection, and he's giving them to ME? Would this have happened if I hadn't gotten rid of my others? Is this the karma nonsense my mother keeps reading about? As Frank pours himself a glass of water, he mumbles something about the importance of a good "musical education." No matter what prompted this act of generosity, it seems like Frank just wanted to give my music career a little nudge. Like Ryan said, maybe I need to trust in the universe a little more.

"You in a band?" Frank asks.

I tell him I used to be.

"Gotta start another one soon," he says. "That's how you learn to be a musician, being in a band."

And right then and there I know exactly where I'll be tomorrow—at the Guitar Center, hanging up a new flyer.

He spots my guitar and picks it up. IS FRANK ZAPPA GOING TO PLAY MY GUITAR? Sure enough, he leans back and lets my Gibson WAIL. It's not a piece I recognize, just something intricate and wonderful he makes up on the spot. This is hands down the best moment of my life—and that includes kissing Caroline for the first time.

I am eternally grateful he doesn't ask me to play and just returns my guitar to its stand. I thank Frank profusely for the records and the private performance and follow him outside. He tells me to call him when I finish the next batch of transcriptions, then heads to the bottom of the driveway.

"You're walking?" I ask.

"My friend dropped me off with his truck. I don't live far."

I feel stupid offering Zappa a ride on my bike, but that's exactly what I do. He gives a little smirk when I point to the back of my banana seat.

"Think you can pedal us both up the hill?"

Just like life has a soundtrack, it has a constant stream of images too. I get a flash of the first photograph Caroline took of me that day in my room, the Vietnamese girl running from a napalm attack, then my family sitting at the kitchen table having dinner together, not knowing it was one of the very last times. I take a mental picture as if from high above Laurel Canyon—me pedaling up the dirt road, Frank Zappa holding on as I do. And the music to accompany this image? It's original and loud and exciting—I just haven't written it yet.

You Asked for It, You Got It: Quinn's List of the Most Important Albums of All Time— in no particular order

★ Revolver—The Beatles

★ The Freewheelin' Bob Dylan—Bob Dylan

★ Who's Next—The Who

★ Pet Sounds—The Beach Boys

★ The Velvet Underground & Nico—The Velvet Underground & Nico

★ Sticky Fingers—The Rolling Stones

★ Abraxas—Santana

★ Music from Big Pink—The Band

★ Are You Experienced—Jimi Hendrix

★ Sgt. Pepper's Lonely Hearts Club Band—The Beatles

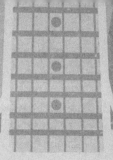

★ **Led Zeppelin IV**—Led Zeppelin

★ **Blue**—Joni Mitchell

★ **Tommy**—The Who

★ **Live at the Apollo**—James Brown

★ **Liege and Lief**—Fairport Convention

★ **Disraeli Gears**—Cream

★ **Highway 61 Revisited**—Bob Dylan

★ **The Doors**—The Doors

★ **Tumblewead Connection**—Elton John

★ **Abbey Road**—The Beatles

★ **Elvis Presley**—Elvis Presley

★ **The Beatles** (aka **The White Album**)—The Beatles

★ **Freak Out!**—Frank Zappa and the Mothers of Invention

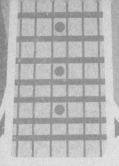

★ **Crosby, Stills & Nash**—Crosby, Stills & Nash

★ **The Notorious Byrd Brothers**—The Byrds

★ **Surrealistic Pillow**—Jefferson Airplane

★ **Cheap Thrills**—Janis Joplin with Big Brother & the Holding Company

★ **Led Zeppelin II**—Led Zeppelin

★ **What's Going On**—Marvin Gaye

★ **Something/Anything?**—Todd Rundgren

★ **Johnny Cash at Folsom Prison**—Johnny Cash

★ **Paranoid**—Black Sabbath

★ **Sweetheart of the Rodeo**—The Byrds

★ **The Rise and Fall of Ziggy Stardust & the Spiders from Mars**—David Bowie

★ **Moondance**—Van Morrison

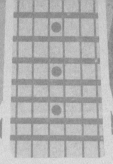

★ **I Never Loved a Man the Way I Love You**—Aretha Franklin

★ **Tapestry**—Carole King

★ **L.A. Woman**—The Doors

★ **After the Gold Rush**—Neil Young

★ **The Gilded Palace of Sin**—The Flying Burrito Brothers

★ **Tea for the Tillerman**—Cat Stevens

★ **Exile on Main Street**—The Rolling Stones

★ **American Beauty**—The Grateful Dead

For those of you who say this is too many albums to be stranded with on a desert island, I say that having these records would be more important than anything else, including food, water, and a boat. Just don't forget the turntable.

AUTHOR'S NOTE

The songs, albums, photographs, and events in this novel were tirelessly researched—although I have to admit, Googling what month Deep Purple's *Machine Head* was released straddles the line between work and procrastination. I knowingly bent only one fact for the purpose of my fiction: during the time Frank Zappa was hanging out with Quinn in Laurel Canyon, in real life he spent a chunk of that time in a wheelchair, recuperating from falling fifteen feet off a London stage when a crazed fan took a run at him. I hated to put poor Frank through that again and wanted to keep the 1971–72 time line to work Nick Ut's photo into the story. As Quinn says, if you haven't seen that picture, please try to find it. Forty years later, it's just as devastating. General William Westmoreland—head of military operations during most of the Vietnam War—gave a speech years afterward saying it looked like the girl in the photo had been involved in "a hibachi accident" (*Washington Post*, January 19, 1986). Really, General Westmoreland? Is that what's going on in that picture? And since the Afghan war is now the longest running war in U.S. history, I thought looking at the draft was important subject matter, too. But of course, writing this book was also a great excuse to crank up some classic rock and roll. So sit back, turn it up to eleven, and enjoy.

Illustrations in This Book

About the Author

JANET TASHJIAN is a longtime music buff, who can recognize almost any song within the first two notes. She still has her old albums (that she bought with the money she earned babysitting) in addition to cassettes and CDs, as well as thousands of digital downloads. She can't imagine living in a world without music.

The author of many acclaimed novels, including The Gospel According to Larry, Vote for Larry, Larry and the Meaning of Life, and Fault Line, Janet Tashjian also collaborated on My Life as a Book and My Life as a Stuntboy with her son, Jake. She lives with her family in Los Angeles, California, not far from Laurel Canyon.

janettashjian.com